STARRY NIGHT

Martin Waddell is widely regarded as one of the finest contemporary writers of books for young people. He has won many awards and was Ireland's nominee for the prestigious Hans Christian Andersen Award in 2000. Among his many titles are the novels *Tango's Baby*, *The Life and Loves of Zoë T. Curley* and *The Kidnapping of Suzie Q*. One of a trilogy of books set in Northern Ireland, *Starry Night* won the Other Award, was runner-up for the Guardian Children's Fiction Award and was shortlisted for the Young Observer Teenage Fiction Prize. The other books in the trilogy are *The Beat of the Drum* and *Frankie's Story*. Martin Waddell lives with his wife Rosaleen in Newcastle, County Down, Northern Ireland.

Books by the same author

Frankie's Story
The Beat of the Drum
Tango's Baby
The Kidnapping of Suzie Q
The Life and Loves of Zoë T. Curley

CHAPTER ONE

"Kathleen? Kathleen?"

I could hear Mammy calling, but I paid no heed. I was up in my own hidey-hole, in the barn, lying in the straw dreaming, and I knew what she'd be after.

Why is it always me?

"Come here this minute, Kathleen!" Mammy yelled.

I stuck my head up over the straw. She was limping round the yard in her big boots, with the pig bucket in one hand, and Imelda in the other. She didn't sound too pleased.

There was no getting out of it.

I left my dream, and hopped down the sacks out into the yard, and the sun. Way down the low field the lake was glinting in the light. Our house at Kiltarragh is a grand place to be in the summer, if only you could get some peace in it. Some hopes!

"Take this child out of my way, Kathleen,"

Mammy said, wagging the bucket at me.

"What for?" I said.

"Never you mind what for," she said. "Take her down the fields till he's gone."

"Who is 'he'?" I said.

"The Monkey's Uncle!" she said. In other words, she wasn't telling me. "Do as I say, before I brain you with this bucket."

"OK," I said. "Come'n, Imelda, and we'll go see the cow."

"Put the boots on her," Mammy said. "The low field is no better than a sheugh."

I put the boots on Imelda and took her out over the wall, down the track towards the low field. Our Frank will drain it someday, he says, but he is taking his time getting it done.

Mammy watched us over the wall, making sure we were going. I had the thought that it was *me* she wanted rid of, not the child, but I put it behind me.

Mammy isn't like that. If she wants rid of you she tells you so, most times. It's funny to see her do it, because she is small, but she goes around giving orders like Napoleon.

"There's the cow," I told Imelda.

Imelda looked at it. "So 'tis," she said, not sounding very impressed.

"The cow has a calf in her," I explained to Imelda. "That is why your daddy has her in the low field, away from the other ones. She is all fat."

"Like Auntie Rose," Imelda said.

"Don't let Rose hear you saying that," I said.

8

"Auntie Rose is all fat, like the cow," Imelda said. "My mammy says so. That's how I know it."

Trust Carmel. You would think she could keep her big mouth shut with personal remarks like that, in front of the child. Our Rose is a big girl all right, but Carmel's no one to be talking. You should see *her* backside in the jeans! Carmel is married to our Frank, and they have the rent of Quinn's old house down the lane. Not that the Quinns would recognize it, after Carmel was in it a week.

I heard a car in the lane, and then I caught a glimpse of it, going past Regans', bouncing down into the dip, and pulling up past Carmel's at our house where the lane stops. It was a blue Renault.

Would it be Father Boyle, or the canon? Then I knew it wouldn't be, because they have smart cars, and this one was all rusty down one wing.

Frank must have seen the car too, for he was heading down the spud field to the back door. Maybe Frank was on about renting Ryan's fields and raising money to do it.

"Kathleen!" Imelda wailed.

I turned round.

"Och jeepers! *Imelda,*" I said.

She was sitting in the muck, and when I yelled her face crumpled like a bun and her mouth twitched down at the corners.

"Och Imelda, look at you!" I said. "Get up out of that."

I got her to her feet. She'd sat in a gift the cow

had left for her.

"It's all down your dress and pants," I told her.

The dress wasn't too much of a stink, but the pants were. If I took her back to Carmel's like that, Carmel would skin me. The way Carmel goes on when anything happens to the child you could forget I'm the unpaid baby-sitter round the place all the school holidays – *my* holidays – while she's off in Dundalk three days a week earning the keep of her car. I have no holidays at all, for if it isn't baby-minding Imelda it's helping Mammy round the house, or fixing the hedges for Frank, all summer long. That's when our Teresa and Rose are on at the soap factory. When they're laid off it isn't so bad, but Guess Who still gets landed with the dirty work.

"Take your pants off, Imelda," I told her, and she did.

"We'll give them a dip in the lake," I said. I took her by the hand and we went over that way, skirting the bog holes.

"You sit there, Imelda," I told her, sitting her down on Daddy's rock, and I took the pants and rinsed the muck off in our nice clean sunshiny lake. I put them on the rock to dry, well spread out, and then I had a look at Imelda.

The muck was on the end of her dress, but only just, and it was down the back of both legs, and on her boots. She must have bombed the cow's gift bang in the middle.

"Come on," I said. "We'll take you to the tap."

We cut across the stone way, and out into the lane, then up past Regans'.

Mrs Regan was in the yard, wouldn't you know, pretending she was just about going to do something, but couldn't remember what.

I knew she'd seen us coming across the stone way.

"Katie, is it?" Mrs Regan said.

Nobody else calls me Katie and lives, but Mrs Regan always does it, just for the pleasure of annoying me.

"And Frank's chick," she said, looking at Imelda. Imelda hid behind me.

"That's a grand child," Mrs Regan said. "Takes after your side of the family."

"Yes, Mrs Regan," I said, wondering if she was having a dig at Carmel. Every other word Mrs Regan says is a dig at somebody, starting with the Pope and running down to her Patsy.

"You'd know Frank was her father," Mrs Regan said. "She has a look of the Fays."

"Yes, Mrs Regan," I said.

"Fine head of hair on her," Mrs Regan said. "Dark as the night."

She gave me a look. She *was* getting at something. Maybe it was Carmel. Carmel had something done to her hair, but it didn't wash on right. She has to keep doing it with a bottle. The Fays are all dark, except me. I think I'm a mousy-haired throwback.

"Was that Frank in a new car I saw going up the

lane to your place?" she said, making it sound casual, although she was all ears to know. She *knew* it wasn't Frank.

"Frank's got no new car, Mrs Regan," I said. It's Carmel has the new car, because she needs it for going into her work in Dundalk. Carmel is on the pig's back. She signs on unemployed in the North, and then nips over the border to Dundalk where she has her part-time job, and nobody any the wiser. Kiltarragh townland is just the wrong side of the border, which is why we have all the soldiers running around. If our land was the other side of the road we would be in the Republic, instead of Northern Ireland.

"I wondered who would be going up the lane, this time of the day," Mrs Regan said.

"Aye, you would!" I said, giving her back as good as I got.

She picked it up, like a flash.

"Would what?" she said.

"Wonder," I said, and I left it there, between us.

Mrs Regan has her nose into everything, and particularly into Frank and Carmel, because Frank is making a go of things round the place, not like Patsy Regan. It serves Mrs Regan right that she's married to Patsy, for they're a pair.

"You should away and see to your visitor," Mrs Regan said.

"Yes, Mrs Regan," I said, and I kept on walking.

I wasn't going to give her the pleasure of knowing that I didn't know who our visitor was. It was none of her business what I did or didn't know.

I put her out of my mind, and concentrated on how grand it was, going up the lane, with the sun nipping down between the bushes and the branches overhead. It was a green tunnel, in a dream, with a crock of gold at the end of it for Imelda, and a big hunky prince for me!

No gold.

No prince.

I got Imelda up to the stand tap in the yard at Carmel's.

"Going to have a shower bath!" I told Imelda, and she thought it was great. She's a dote, Imelda.

Carmel doesn't leave me the key when she goes off, and she's not one for leaving the house open, so I had nothing proper to dry Imelda with. I was wondering what I would do about it when Frank came down the lane from our house.

"Daddy!" said Imelda.

Maybe he didn't hear her. I don't know. Anyway, he cut past us, up over the wall and into the field, with a face like thunder.

Whatever had been happening at our house, Frank wasn't pleased. It's not like him to cut the child.

"Your daddy didn't see you, Imelda," I told her, and I got an old blanket from the barn and dried her off with that. I was busy putting the dress back on her when the Renault went bumping by, but I couldn't make out who was driving it, worse luck.

Mrs Regan would know this time sure enough,

because of the racket the Renault made bumping down the lane. The rocking of the Renault was loud enough to be heard a mile away. Mrs Regan would be out in her yard again, taking a good look at the driver.

The lane is a good lane up as far as Carmel has to drive her car, our Teresa says, and after that Frank couldn't be bothered. I think our Teresa is right. Frank is grand, but he's slow enough about doing things, or he was until Carmel got her claws in him. Teresa says Carmel is heading for trouble the way she keeps after our Frank. Carmel should have known what he was like before she married him, and not pester him so much for this and that. All I know is Carmel gets what she wants, and we don't.

I went up to our house.

"Is the visitor gone, Mammy?" I said. I knew there was only one visitor because I saw that much when the car was passing.

"Aye, and our good name with him!" said Mammy, and she limped off into the house. Mammy has a bad leg, and it gives her gip. Teresa says Mammy is getting like an old woman with her troubles to bear, these days, but I don't see much change. She's the same as she always was, only a bit slower out of bed; and some days she has me running after her with forgetting things … other days she doesn't. She can remember well enough when it suits her.

I took Imelda into the front room, out of her

way. I could hear Mammy trailing round in the kitchen, and poking at the range, but I didn't go in to her.

To tell the truth, my nose was out of joint. It's not like Mammy and Frank to have secrets on me, as if I was a child, like Imelda. Now I'm grown up, Mammy talks to me a lot. If it was only one of their rows about buying land, then there was no need to run me off the place. I had a feeling it was more than that. Frank was upset, and Mammy was worse, and whatever they were on about, they were keeping me out of it.

Mind you, that was one way of making sure that I'd have a big go at finding out.

CHAPTER TWO

Wanting to find out was one thing, and finding out was another.

I dropped enough hints, but nobody was talking.

That evening I had the notion that I might learn a bit more outside our place than I would in it, so I went off to O'Connor's by-the-way to see if Ann was going to the disco in the hall, but with the plain purpose of seeing what the gossip was. Ann's Aunt Mary is a clatterbox but as my luck would have it she wasn't around. Ann didn't want to go to the dance. She says the canon's disco is for weirdos. I only go the odd time when I've got nothing better to do. Ann wanted to sit in and watch TV, so I sat in with her.

The O'Connors have two colour TVs and a portable, *and* a video.

Brendan Prince was on TV with his band, and Ann wanted to video him. She's mad on country and western.

"He's all hairy," I told her, when Brendan Prince was on, and she wasn't pleased. He was singing like a cowboy from Texas, when everybody knows he is all the way from Limerick on the CIE bus to Dublin.

"He's g-r-e-a-t!" she said, hugging on to a cushion. We had to watch it again, when he was over.

"I wouldn't mind him riding up the lane on a big white horse," Ann said.

"Hairy git!" I said, and she came after me with the cushion. She was bashing me when her Aunt Mary put her head round the door and told her to stop it this instant.

I thought she'd come in and her tongue would start, but it didn't happen. She was taken odd. She hardly said a word to me. I was glad to get out of the place.

Ann said she'd walk with me, so we went out and down O'Connor's field to the lakeside. Our house is up the other side of the lake. Our fields are one side, and they have the other, but James O'Connor has the fishing rights. Much good may it do him, for there are no fish.

"Is your aunt off-colour?" I asked Ann.

"Nope," she said.

"She hadn't much chat," I said.

Ann didn't say anything, so I thought I'd better give up the detective work and try another tack. If the O'Connors knew what was going on at our place, nobody was saying. I had a feeling maybe they *did* know, or the aunt did anyway. Ann might

17

not know, being a stranger. Ann comes down from Belfast every summer, and we're pals. I'm almost the only one round here she has any time for, that is what she says. Ann's nice, but there are a lot of things about Kiltarragh that she doesn't understand and anyway she's not like her Aunt Mary. I'd trust Ann to keep a secret, if I had one – only this time, I could have wished she was more of a gossip.

"I like your aunt's house," I said to Ann, just to get out of the awkwardness of nothing being said.

"Do you?" she said, sounding surprised.

"She's got nice things," I said.

"I suppose so," she said, with a shrug.

Ann is used to those things. New things. We have hardly any new things in our house, and there's such a lot of us, with Mammy and Rose and Teresa and me *and* our Mike all under the one roof, when Mike isn't away at the building in London. There ought to be money with Rose and Teresa working, but there isn't. They've got rotten jobs in the soap factory, and half the time they are laid off.

"When I get married I'll have nice things," I said. "I have it all worked out." I have, too. I know the things I want to have. I've been over and over it in my mind, lying on my own up in my hidey-hole at the barn.

"What do you want to get married *for*?" Ann said. "To get nice things?" The way she said it, it sounded all wrong.

"Not for that," I said, because I didn't want her

to think I would marry any old somebody just because he had money. I'm busy working on the sort of somebody I want to marry, but so far it hasn't come out right.

"I'm not getting married," Ann announced. "I'm going to get a job and have a career of my own, and I won't get married unless I have to."

"*Have* to?" I said.

"You *know*," she said awkwardly, giving me a funny look.

Then she tried to make a laugh of it. "Me and my big mouth," she blurted out.

"You wouldn't want your Auntie Mary to hear you saying things like that," I said.

"I don't care," said Ann. "You've only got to look at her to see where marriage gets you."

I think she was only saying it. The O'Connors are all right. Ann's Uncle James is a builder and they have piles and piles of money, which is how they get the nice things. Ann's father and mother are teachers in Belfast, so I suppose that's where Ann gets her funny ideas from. She comes out with some terrible things.

We were down by the lakeside, sitting on my daddy's rock. Rose told me he used to sit there, by the deep side of the lake. You can see the water is deep. It was dark and gleamy with the dusk, and sucking against the reeds. Real romantic ... all I needed was somebody to be romantic with, but that sort are in short order round Kiltarragh. I don't know anybody I'd want to marry, even if I could.

19

"I'm not going to live in a place like this," Ann said hurriedly. Obviously she wanted off the subject in case I'd go telling her Auntie Mary the way she was talking. "This place is deadly."

"What do you come here for, if you think it is so deadly?" I asked.

"I have to come here to please my daddy," she said. "It's supposed to be my holidays."

"It's not so bad," I said, thinking I ought to stick up for it. Kiltarragh is my own place, and a better place than Belfast any day. I couldn't sit there and let a stranger run our place down.

"When you're older you'll want out of here," Ann said. "You ought to think about it. You could go to Belfast and do teacher training or something."

"I might," I said. "It depends."

"You're smart enough," she said. "All you have to do is work a bit for your exams. Anybody can do it."

Anybody like Ann can. I bet I'd not qualify for teacher training even if I wanted to. And *why* should I want to? I looked down in the water at me looking up, and I agreed with myself.

"You could do it, Kathleen, honest!" Ann urged me.

"Who'd look after Mammy?" I said.

"Your Teresa would," she said.

"Or Rose," I said. "Only they couldn't. They've got jobs."

"Those aren't *jobs*," Ann said. "Cooped up all

day in a factory, watching machines clank. In a year or two there won't be any more jobs like that, even if anybody was fool enough to take them."

"I wouldn't mind a job in the soap," I said. "I mean, it wouldn't be great, but it would do."

"What for?"

"A bit of money," I said. "So I could buy a few things."

"*Things,*" said Ann, as if things were nothings.

"You have things," I said. "I haven't."

"What things?" she said.

"Clothes," I said.

She looked at my clothes, and she looked at hers, and she didn't say anything for a moment. Then she said: "I see what you mean."

It was reasonable of her. She could have told me the old hand-me-downs Rose took up for me were dandy, but Ann isn't like that. She was honest with me. She knew that her clothes came from posh Belfast shops, and mine were dropping off me.

"Money isn't everything," was the best she could manage.

"It sure helps," I said.

"If you're going to be moody, I'm going back to the house," Ann said, but she didn't say it meanly. She's a real friend, one you can talk to, not like Carmel. Rose is the other one I talk to, but she's nearly thirty now, and it isn't the same as somebody my own age. Rose is grand, but she doesn't know how to treat me now I'm not a baby round the place. She was always after me when I was wee and now she's confused about it. Half the time I'm her pal and the other half I'm somebody who needs looking after. Rose *is* special but she's my sister, she didn't pick me for a friend.

We went back to O'Connor's. Ann made me coffee and we had it downstairs. Her Aunt Mary came in but she didn't talk much this time, either, and when she did, she didn't *say* anything. I don't know if Ann noticed. It was very odd, and gave me an uncomfortable feeling.

I went away, convinced that Mary O'Connor knew something. She'd tell Ann what it was when I was gone, and if she did I might ask Ann straight out … and then again, I might not.

It was difficult for me with strangers maybe knowing about something that was going on at our house, and me not knowing what it was. Then again, maybe there was nothing to know, and Mary O'Connor had a cold in her head or what-ever – not that that ever made her stop talking before.

Rose was out looking for me when I came up the low field to our yard. By-the-way she was pumping up her bike, but I knew she was looking out for me.

"Where've you been?" she said.

"O'Connor's," I said.

"Time you were in your bed," she said, in her bossy mood.

It was on the tip of my tongue to tell her I was no Imelda, and that she had no call to be after me like a clucking hen. I'm almost fifteen, but sometimes Rose treats me like her baby. I was going to say it, but then I buttoned up. It was nice of her to be worried about me.

Just then there was a din, an old whirry 'copter in the sky. It came in low over the house, like a big daddy-long-legs.

"The army's out again," I said.

It whirred past us, and up over the fields beyond, leaving its throb behind it in the whins.

"*Bed,*" said Rose.

I went up the stairs, and into my room. I have a room of my own now, since Frank put up the partition. I have my bed in it, and the washstand, and an old car seat out of Frank's car for a sit-me-down, and a pair of curtains to put on the window when Mike makes me a window; *when* Mike makes me my window will depend on when he gets back from London. I have no window yet, just the gaps in the slates, and two buckets for the rain coming through. The nicest thing in my room is the bedspread Rose made for me when I was just a child. There's every colour in it, like a rainbow. It's all bits-and-pieces-patchwork. She must have worked on it forever.

I got in beneath my rainbow spread, and put on the radio. Ann gave me the radio when she got a new one. She brought it all the way down from Belfast for me. Many another one wouldn't bother about somebody living in a bog, but Ann does.

I wish I was like Ann.

23

I wish I had clothes and houses and other things to think about, not just will-it-be-a-bad-year-for-the-spuds and Mammy's sick leg.

I wish…

…I don't know what I wish.

I lay there listening to my radio, walking my fingers up and down the underside of the slates. The head of my bed is right in beneath the roof. The slates were still warm from the heat of the day, and I could see the sky through the chinks.

I thought I wouldn't get to sleep because the bit of me that likes making up stories was hard at work on our visitor, Mammy's bit about "our good name", Frank going past down the lane so mad that he didn't even stop for Imelda, and the queer way Mary O'Connor acted.

Perhaps it was money trouble again, like the time Frank had the man from the bank loans over. Only the man from the bank loans had a decent car, not a beat-up old Renault.

Or maybe the social security were on to Carmel, and her job in Dundalk.

Carmel is a bad one. Teresa says Carmel is mad as hell when Frank does things for us, but Carmel will just have to learn to live with it. She was glad enough to get her feet under Frank's table in the first place.

If Carmel was arrested and put in jail for having a job in the South and signing on unemployed in the North we'd be back to being just us. One family and one house, Rose and Mammy and

Teresa and Frank and Mike and me and wee Imelda. We'd look after Imelda for Frank – well, I know who'd get the child-minding, as usual.

I had myself half convinced the trouble was over Carmel – but the other half wasn't listening.

I gave it up, and went back to thinking about being married in my bungalow, but my own nice dream wouldn't work out for me, not this time.

The other business, whatever it was, kept breaking through the dream, and it wouldn't go away.

CHAPTER THREE

I don't know what it was that woke me up, but there I was, awake. Maybe it was the old whirry 'copter coming back for more soldiers, or maybe it was just one of those feelings you get, when something is wrong in a house.

I knew there was some reason I was awake, something that wasn't right, only I couldn't figure out what it was.

I went out to the landing.

There was a light on downstairs, and somebody moving about.

I went down.

There's a small window in our door, the door into the kitchen. Frank took the back door of the house off and put on a new one, and when he'd changed the back door he got rid of the one at the foot of the stairs and put the old back door on in its place. That is why there is a window in it, the way there wouldn't be in most people's inside doors.

Teresa put a plastic curtain on it, but the plastic is curled up, so you can see through.

Rose was in the kitchen, all hunkered up on the sofa in her dressing-gown, the one Teresa bought her because it had roses on it. She had her floppy slippers on and she was smoking a cigarette.

She's not supposed to be smoking.

Frank said he'd tan her hide for her if he caught her smoking.

She was smoking just the same.

She was smoking quick puffs and pulls, and flicking the ash down into a saucer, which she had on the arm of the sofa beside her.

I didn't know what I was at, spying on her, but I'd started doing it, and now it was difficult to get out of it. If I went back up the stairs she'd hear me on the creaky step. I thought I'd be best to walk in on her, but I hesitated for fear I'd put my foot in it.

There was something wrong about Rose, and the way she was smoking her cigarette, grabbing puffs and blowing the smoke out of her nose.

I'd never seen anyone blowing smoke out of their nose before like that.

Maybe she had cancer. Our Rose had cancer and that was what all the secrecy was about! It would be awful, if it was that.

It wasn't that. That was just me making up stories again.

I took my thimbleful of courage in my hands, and knocked on the door. I don't know why I

27

knocked, because it is our own kitchen door and everybody comes in and out without a by-your-leave, but I did anyway.

"Who's that?" she said.

"Only me," I said, opening the door, and sticking my head round the crack.

The ciggy was in the hand she had curled, so it must have been burning her. She moved the cushion round to cover the saucer that she was using as her ash-tray.

"You're a nice one to be up," she said. "You should be in your bed."

"I couldn't sleep," I said.

"You were asleep half an hour ago," Rose said. She must have been in to check me, as if I was a wee child. She always used to do that. I didn't know she was still doing it.

"I heard you up, and I thought I'd come down," I said.

The smoke was in the air, but I never made mention of it.

"Checking up on me?" she said, getting to her feet.

Well, I *was*, but I wasn't going to say so.

She went over to the range and opened the fire to look in, by-the-way seeing if it was slacked. I deliberately didn't watch her, but I know the ciggy went in. When I looked back she was massaging the palm of her hand.

Her face was all puffy and red, and it wasn't the fire.

"Is anything the matter, Rose?" I said, straight out. If I couldn't ask her a question like that, who could?

She didn't *look* as if she'd got cancer, or was dying, or anything.

"Divil the bit," she said, trying to laugh it off.

I never said a word.

"Nothing 'Our Rose' can't cope with!" she said.

So there *was* something.

"One of these days, we'll have a wee yarn," she said. "One of these days, but not tonight. All right?"

"Why not tonight?" I said.

"Because ... because tonight I'm playing your game, hiding away and having a good long think," she said. "Some other time, when I have it all sorted out, we'll have a talk, you wait and see."

Then she gave me a hug, and sent me off back up the stairs, like I was Imelda.

I was all jumbled up inside.

It hadn't just been me making up things to scare myself. Something was going on. Maybe it was Carmel making more trouble with Frank. Or something the matter with Mike, over in England. Or maybe it was Rose herself. I was big enough to know about it, whatever it was, but even Rose wouldn't tell me.

Rose wasn't long after me coming up the stairs, but long enough I suppose to dispose of the saucer with the ash in it, so it wouldn't be there for

Mammy or Teresa to tell Frank about.

No mess in the morning, except whatever mess it was that I wasn't supposed to know about.

CHAPTER FOUR

I was up early for the cows and when I got back Rose was already off to early Mass, packed in the car with Frank and Carmel and Imelda, so I didn't get the chance to have another go at her.

Mammy was in the kitchen, waiting for me to do her leg. I always do it, because Mammy says I'm the one with the touch.

"You should be in to see Dr Mallon with that, Mammy," Teresa said from the table, where she was tucking into her bacon.

"Och, withers!" said Mammy.

She has an ulcer on the leg, really nasty, and it is one of my jobs to put the ointment on, and change the bandage for her.

"You need treatment," Teresa said. She was just stirring it up. She knows the way Mammy is about doctors. Teresa is like that sometimes, as though she needed a bit of a row with somebody to keep her going.

"I'm falling apart at the seams," Mammy said cheerfully, and then she let out a yowl, for I'd tweaked a soft spot.

"Carmel would take you down to Mass in the car," Teresa said. "You know she would."

"I want no charity from her ladyship," Mammy said, real stiff.

Maybe the trouble was Carmel. Carmel told Teresa one time that Frank should have a farm of his own, but where would Frank get the money? Carmel wants to get away from us, that's the thing, but there is no way Frank will go, because he looks after us and we look after him. That's the way it is, and Carmel has no call to be complaining about her house, and wanting things all her own way. We got on well before Carmel came.

"That Carmel one has a hard face on her," I said.

"Hold your tongue!" said Teresa.

"The child is right," said Mammy.

"You've no call to be snappy at me!" said Teresa, sharply, and she went off upstairs to get dressed for Mass.

"Old humpy," Mammy said, wagging her head at the sound of Teresa going up the stairs.

"Everybody is humpy around the house these days," I said.

"Well, I'm not," said Mammy. "Come here, wee baby, and give the old Mammy a hug." She's an awful old cuddler, Mammy.

"Was Carmel giving off at you about the child's

clothes?" she said, when we'd finished our hug. "Never you mind if she does. A bit of honest dirt never hurt anyone."

"Sometimes I wish Carmel would go away," I said.

"Frank's made his bed," said Mammy. "He may lie in it."

"I'm awful sorry for Frank, sometimes," I said.

"It's time you were getting dressed for eleven o'clock Mass," Mammy said, as if I'd never said anything.

"Are you not going to Mass yourself?" I said.

"Frank'll take me to the late," she said.

"Teresa would run you down with us in Frank's old car," I said. "Wouldn't that be better, and not bothering Frank a second time?"

"Frank'll look after me," she said.

I was put out, for if Mammy had been going we could have had Frank's old car, but without her it was me and Teresa for the road.

We got out our bikes.

"Could we not take Frank's car anyway?" I said to Teresa.

"I'd not be beholden to our Frank," said Teresa, and that was that, only now I was certain sure what the trouble was. Carmel had been at Frank about the farm again, and Frank had had some man up to Mammy to get her to sign papers, and Mammy wasn't doing it. Why should she? The farm belongs to Mammy, and there is no way she'd let that Carmel one get it. No wonder Teresa was mad at Carmel for causing ructions round the place. I was well pleased with myself for working it out.

We pedalled off down the lane and the bumps of the old bike nearly had the backside off me.

"That lane is a terror," I told Teresa, when we were past Regans' and on to Carmel's new lane.

"Sure is," said Teresa.

She had her brown coat on, and her hat, and her brown shoes. She looked a sight on Mike's old bike.

I think she knew it too, because she got off the bike at Tully's, where she put it in the hedge. Then she got her beads and her missal out of the saddle-bag, straightened the hat, and hoofed it down the road to the church.

Carmel drove past, going home, and gave us a toot on the horn as she went by. I waved, but Teresa never even turned her head. Imelda gave me a wave out of the back. Carmel always dresses them up to the nines for Sunday Mass – you should see Frank in his suit.

What was Rose doing in the car with them, when everybody else was mad at Carmel and Frank for causing trouble? She'd never take Carmel's side of things, would she?

I spent half the Mass thinking about it, and I said a prayer that Carmel would wise up and stop making trouble.

I lost Teresa coming out, and then I spotted her down at the bottom of the graveyard, visiting Daddy.

Daddy is down there, with his mother and Bernie. My sister Bernadette died when she was three. She would have made six of us Fays, and two miscarries.

Mammy still cries for Bernie, the odd time.

"Do you want a lift home?" Ann said to me, bouncing over from the crowd round her Uncle James.

"I have the bike," I told her, though I wouldn't have minded a ride in James O'Connor's new car. It is well seen that somebody makes money house-building, even if it isn't our Mike. "Anyway, I'm in no hurry home, for Carmel is up to her tricks again."

"Oh?" said Ann, and I told her what was going on.

"So that's what the trouble was," Ann said. "Good."

"Good?" I said.

She hesitated a minute, and then she said. "I just thought it might have been something worse."

Something *worse*? The way she said it, I had the feeling there *was* something worse, but I didn't get the chance to ask her because of the crowd coming out of the church. Teresa was headed for us up the path from the grave, with her head down and her hands folded in front of her.

"I think she's a sad person," said Ann.

"I think so too," I said.

Teresa is nice-looking, if only she would show it. It is the way she walks that stops her, and the way she buttons herself up inside her clothes. You

35

wouldn't think it was summer to see Teresa in her coat and hat and scarf.

"She should have been a nun," Ann said. "She's great nun material."

I don't think Ann is much bothered about nuns. My Auntie Margaret is a nun, and she's a laugh sometimes.

"One of those nuns that whip themselves," Ann said.

"Give over," I said, for fear that Father Riley or the canon would hear us.

I needn't have bothered. The two priests were all in a huddle with James O'Connor, and just at that moment Father Riley let out a bray like a donkey and jumped back, almost knocking our Teresa off her feet.

"Did I trip you, Father?" Teresa said.

"Och no, Teresa," he said, and dived back into the chat.

"*Did I trip you, Father?*" Ann said, mocking Teresa.

"She has a thing about priests," I said.

"Didn't I tell you she should have been a nun?" Ann said.

Teresa came picking her way across to us, her thin face lit up with a kind of blush.

"I'm off," Ann said. "See you." And she disappeared into the crowd.

Teresa and I went for the bikes, finding our way round the men at the gates.

The soldiers were just up the road from the

church, watching the men, and the men were busy not watching them. The soldiers had their wagon pulled in by the side of the road, looking for somebody they could pick up. The men at the gate were acting as if the soldiers weren't there at all, but it could have gone nasty easy enough if the soldiers had tried anything.

"Was there any trouble last night, Teresa?" I said. We'd crossed the road, and gone up past the wagon, and then we crossed back again, never even looking at them. Why should we? It's not their country.

"Nothing but the usual," Teresa said.

We rode home.

It was a great morning for a bike. The hills were green around us and the whins flaring yellow and even with Teresa making heavy weather of pedalling in front of me I couldn't help but think how nice it was.

Maybe one day the soldiers would go away, and then we would be happy. I'd have met the somebody – whoever he was – that I was going to meet and we'd be just us, in the sun, with the new bungalow and the new things and lots and lots more to dream about and do, instead of being stuck with the soldiers and the trouble and Mammy's leg and Carmel not sorting with our ones. It was no morning for old bother like that, for none of it had anything to do with me, and a sunny Sunday, and the bike.

We went by the blast hole at Cone Cross, where

the soldier lost his legs, and up to the crossroads at the foot of our lane.

"I'm wheelin' it," I shouted after Teresa, because I was in no hurry to get back to a house full of rows. She pedalled on, her back stiff against the bumps.

It is three fields to our house from Cone Cross. The house was stuck up there, low and white against the sky.

Despite Frank and Carmel making trouble, I was feeling great, and filled up with hope. Maybe I could go to Belfast like Ann said, and do teacher training, or maybe I could stay and just drink up the sunny days till my hunky prince came by … either road, I was happy inside for a crowd of silly reasons, that were no reasons at all. It is hard *not* to be happy, sometimes.

Imelda came running down the dip to meet me.

"Hi, baby!" I told her, and I got her up on the saddle of the bike and bumped her over a rough bit. She thought it was great. She was all giggles when Frank came out to meet us, and she begged off the bike and up on to his shoulder.

"There you are now," Frank said, settling her with a leg round each side of his neck.

"Imelda is Daddy's girl," I said.

"Indeed she is," said Frank.

I had a funny feeling, a moment of jealousy. I used to be the baby about the place, because they were all grown up before I began. Time was when Frank had *me* up on his shoulders, walking round the fields on a sunny Sunday.

Jealous of Imelda!

Frank was the best brother anybody could hope to get, before Carmel nailed him. It was "wee Kathleen" this and "wee Kathleen" that, and rides on the tractor he borrowed from Joe McMullan – and then I grew up, and Frank got wed.

"How's wee Kathleen today?" he said, as if he could read my thoughts.

"I'm getting to be a big girl," I said.

"You're both my great girls," he said. "You and Imelda."

In that minute, stepping up the lane, I wished I was.

It was dark in the house after the sunlight outside, but Mammy had the table laid, and the pots on the range, and the tea stewing.

Imelda ran off, and there was just me and Frank.

He had his suit and tie on, and his black shoes, and a grey jumper that Carmel got him in Dundalk with Adidas on the side. I don't think it was meant for wearing under a suit, and anyhow he must have been baked.

"Duty done," he said.

"That is no way to talk about Mass!" I said.

"It leaves the day clear," he said.

Then Rose came in.

But she didn't come in.

She came through the door, saw that Frank was there, and went out again.

"Ha!" Frank said, letting a breath out of him. Then he sat there, looking not too pleased.

"Everybody is humpy round here," I said, not too pleased myself, because I'd just got myself feeling happy, and I didn't want old family rows.

"Poor Rose," he said.

"Uh?"

"Mind you don't be upsetting her," he said, and then he rubbed his hands together and stirred himself out of Daddy's chair, making for the door.

"Is anything the matter with Rose?" I said, suddenly confused.

"It'll all come out in the wash," he said awkwardly, and then he was out of the door.

I stood there for a minute, drinking it in. Then I went out after him, but he was gone – skipped off out of my way!

Imelda and Rose were sitting on the wall, and Rose was giving her the tickles.

I thought about marching up and asking her, but then I remembered what Frank had said. I went off to my own hidey-hole in the barn, and lay down there in the shade, where no one could see me, and I could be a mouse.

It wasn't Carmel everybody was upset about. It was Rose.

I lay looking out through my spy hole in the straw. The wind was stirring the lake, and the whins were bright against the fallen wall of the old house down there, where Mrs Owens used to live. I could hear Imelda giggling in the yard.

Everything was passing me by. Someday I'd be like them, Rose and Teresa, coming up to my thirtieth birthday – and Teresa was more than that. I'd be a grown woman, and trapped at Kiltarragh.

I would if I let me be. I'd no need to be. I could leave school, and go away wherever I wanted – to Ann in Belfast, or over to London with Mike.

Rose was all bouncy, playing with the child, but her legs were thick, and her body thicker, and her big plain nice face had something else behind it as she laughed at Imelda – a loneliness.

Maybe she *had* got some terrible disease. Maybe... I didn't know about the maybes, but whatever it was it couldn't be much worse than the way she was now, stuck at Kiltarragh, and in and out to the soap factory, day after day.

CHAPTER FIVE

It turned out to be an odd afternoon, and one I'd not been expecting.

I'd just had my dinner and finished up doing the dishes with Teresa when Ann O'Connor came over the field. Her mammy and daddy were down from Belfast, and they were taking her for a run, and would I come?

Would I!

Their car was dandy. It had big soft seats and no petrol, for it was diesel. I didn't know teachers had big cars. Maybe Ann was right, and I should be a teacher. Some hopes!

We went over the border and ended up at Tara, the Hill of the Kings. I know all about it, for I was there before with Sister Attracta in the school bus. If I was a king I wouldn't live at Tara, for it is near nowhere. We went down to the Great Hall of the Kings, which isn't there. All that is there is a big dip in the ground. You have to imagine the walls and the roof. Ann's daddy got excited about it and so did Ann, but I didn't. I can see a big dip in a field any day. Then Ann and I went to the shop, and Ann bought herself a guide book.

"What do you want that for?" I said.

"It's the Hill of Tara," she said.

"I know it is the Hill of Tara," I said.

"I'm going to read about it," she said.

I don't know what there was to read about. If it was Paris or someplace like that I might want to read about it.

We drove back over the border and along up to O'Connor's, where we had our tea. Afterwards we went down by the lake, where James O'Connor and Ann's daddy went over to the old house to have a look through the holes where the windows used to be.

"He'll be wanting to take it for the Ulster Folk Museum," Ann said.

"What for?"

"Mud walls," said Ann. "He loves mud walls."

"They'd better keep away from it," I said. "The soldiers might be there."

The soldiers sometimes use it as a hidey-hole, where they can watch the border road, not that you'd see them. They're very clever at getting about the place when they don't want to be seen. Our Teresa almost stepped on one in the lane, one night, and she didn't know who was the worst scared, herself or the soldier. Mind you, it was the soldier who had the gun.

43

"Having the soldiers here is a pest," I said.

Ann didn't say anything.

I told her about Patsy Regan. Patsy found one in the hay, doing his business. Patsy took the pitchfork to him. The soldier called Patsy a lot of dirty names. Patsy wanted to go into the town and report him to the officers, but our Frank talked him out of it. You'd never know what harm might come if the soldiers took against you.

"If we had our united Ireland, there'd be no soldiers," I said. "Why don't they just go home? There's no sense in them running round here waiting to get shot at."

"Och, I don't know," Ann said.

"*What* don't you know?" I said. "The Brits caused the whole bother. If they would just clear out of Ireland we'd have North and South together in one country and it would be fine."

Ann made a face.

"*Everybody* knows that," I said.

"Everybody round here," Ann said. "That's not everybody. There's a lot of people where I come from who want to stay British."

"Then they've no sense," I said.

"How do you know?" she said.

"Sure everybody knows it," I said. "You ask anybody round here and you'll get the same answer. If we get the British out and have a united Ireland then we'll all be happy."

"It's not as easy as that, Kathleen," she said. "If you took a vote on it, you'd lose."

44

"If we can't *vote* them out, we'll *blow* them out," I said. Everybody knows Northern Ireland was set up that way at the beginning, so there would be more Protestants in it than us. That's why *their* Ulster is just six counties, and not the nine counties it used to be. If it was nine counties we'd outvote them. That's the Brits' democracy for you.

"*Would* you?" she said. "Bomb people, I mean?"

"No," I said. "I never bombed anybody. But there's them that would."

"And then you'll all settle down in a Banana Republic," she said.

"The British said that that would happen to the Republic. They thought the Irish couldn't run a country," I said. "But we did it. The Republic is still in business – and some of its business is unfinished."

"The northern bit," said Ann. "The All Ireland Catholic Holy State."

That was a real shaker.

"Are you *for* the Protestants, then?" I said.

"No," Ann said.

"Who are you for then?"

"Ordinary people," she said. "Not men with big drums running Catholics out of the shipyard, and not Irish heroes in behind the hedge with their bombs, waiting to blow other Irishmen to bits."

I couldn't figure it out at all. You'd think Ann was a Brit. I *know* James O'Connor is not a Brit, and James O'Connor is her uncle and her own daddy is his brother. It must be living in Belfast with the Protestants that does it.

Ann went off and left me, and that was hard to take.

I was thinking about what she said, coming back round the low field, on the way home.

She lives up in Belfast. She knows what it is like. How could she not know what it is like? Anybody round here could tell her, anybody at all. *And* they could tell her the cause of it.

Then, when I got back to the house, Mike was back off the boat!

Big celebrations! You couldn't have given Mammy a better present. The years dropped off her.

He got me a clock.

"All the way from Kentish Town," he said, handing it over.

"Where?" I said.

"London," he said. "The bright lights and the Big Smoke."

I don't know what he got me a clock for. You'd think in the whole of London there would be something more interesting than a clock.

"It folds down," he said, and he showed me how to click the case. "It closes up like that, so you can fit it easily into your suitcase."

"I haven't got a suitcase," I said. "I don't need one, for I never go anywhere."

"Och, Kathleen!" he said, and he gave me a grin.

46

He got Mammy a Spanish lace shawl and Teresa an apron and Rose a pair of suede boots that were too big for her and Imelda a big box of sweets.

"Better keep them here," Mammy said. "Or Carmel will have them off her."

Mammy put the sweeties on top of the big cupboard by the range, and Imelda kept going back for another one.

We gave Mike a big tea and then he went off with Carmel and Frank into town. That left Teresa with getting Mammy down to Mass in Frank's old car, and me and Rose to bed Imelda.

I thought I'd get my chance to have a yarn with her at last, and then I'd know the worst. Maybe, whatever it was, it wouldn't be so bad.

We went down the lane to Carmel's house to put the child to bed but Imelda started in, and it was a Starry Night or nothing. That means one of Rose's stories. Rose used to tell me a Starry Night story every night, when I was small. They were daft stories, and every one of them she'd start with "One starry night…" like that, and then she'd chuck in any old blether that came into her head. I must have caught it off her, telling stories, because now I'm the one who gets the job with Imelda.

I put Imelda in bed, and I gave her one about a prince that lived over in the old house by the lake, and the fairies getting him and hiding him up Regans' back for a year and a day, and this girl called Imelda getting him back by dancing for the fairies at the fort. Like I said, it was any old blether.

47

Imelda had three of them out of me, before she went over to sleep with her thumb in her mouth – and a sticky looking thumb it was too, for Rose and I had smuggled her down some of the sweeties from the tin Mike brought her.

When I went back into the big room Rose was watching *Miami Vice* on RTE. We get RTE 1 and 2 great up here, Harlech and Ulster Television, and the BBC, so we are on the pig's back.

"What's that about?" I said, sitting down on Carmel's sofa. It is green, with green and white cushions and a shamrock in the middle of each one.

"Drugs," said Rose. "That one is a pusher and the other one is letting on she's making a pass at him and all the time it is a set-up so they can trap him with the stuff."

The one who was letting on she was making a pass was unbuttoning her blouse.

Rose got up and switched off.

"That's not for the like of you," she said.

"Och Rose!" I said.

"You've time enough for that sort of thing," she said, but in the end I got her to switch the set on again and we got James Last.

I didn't have my yarn with Rose.

I didn't, because all of a sudden I could see what the trouble was.

Imelda had it right.

Rose was getting a bump on her.

I sat there and thought should I ask her, and

48

then I didn't know how to do it. Rose isn't married, but she was lying there with her feet up and her head back, and you couldn't miss what was the matter. She *couldn't* be, but she was.

Just like the cow in the field.

CHAPTER SIX

Rose was going to have a baby.

I didn't know what to think about it. She *was*, I mean, I was certain sure about that, though nobody had said anything.

She could have told me herself.

I didn't think Rose ... I didn't know what to think.

I just went on doing what I always do, though I was desperate to have a talk about it – but who could I talk to? A thing like that is not the sort of thing you'd say, not straight out to somebody. If she wanted to say it to me, she would, in her own time, for it was her business. It wasn't the sort of thing I'd like to say to Teresa or Mammy. They'd know. They'd have to know, there'd be no call to say it, a private thing like that. It would be all right if Rose was getting married ... all right ... sort of ... but not really, what with the neighbours knowing. Mrs Regan and the O'Connors and

50

everybody, knowing about it before me, because I couldn't see what was in front of my face.

I was all confused.

In the morning I went downstairs and did Mammy's leg and the spuds the way I always do, and then I went out in the yard with Imelda.

Ann came over the yard wall.

"Hi," she said.

"How are you?" I said, not too enthusiastic, for I didn't know where I stood with her, after the talk we'd had about the Brits, and there was the other thing, about Rose. She must have known about Rose, she must have noticed. Ann wouldn't miss a thing like that, but she had never let on. Maybe she thought I knew, too.

"'Lo, Ann," said Imelda.

"Hello, baby!" Ann said, and she chased Imelda about a bit, maybe hoping to soften me up that way.

"Coming for a walk?" Ann said.

"I would, only there's her," I said, meaning Imelda.

"Imelda will come for a walk, won't you, baby?" Ann said.

We went up the back lane. Ann had a white blouse, and a flowery skirt, and her sandals on. She looked just like summer. I wished I could talk to her.

"What's the matter?" Ann said.

"Nothing."

"You're all funny this morning."

51

"I'm not."

She hooked a stalk of grass out of the ditch, and began to play with it, between her fingers.

"It is different in Belfast, Kathleen," she said. "The whole Protestant/Catholic thing doesn't look the same to us, up there. It's just not that simple."

"Never mind," I said. I wasn't bothered about that any more. I wanted somebody to talk to about the other thing, but I didn't know how to begin.

"Let's forget it then, and just be friends, eh?" said Ann.

"OK," I said.

We walked on to the top of the lane.

"Grand view," Ann said.

She was right. From the top of our lane you can see most of the county, the fields coloured and patched like the bedspread Rose made, and the hills and the bog road and Wheevey Lake and the humpy line of the Carlingford Mountains in the back of it all.

Imelda kept pottering round us, so I couldn't get saying anything.

We sat down on the grass. The ground was cold. It hadn't heated up yet. I lay back. I thought I could just lie and lie there, and the whole thing would go away. Ann got Imelda working on a daisy chain, and then Imelda wandered off down the field. We lay there watching her.

"You know you were saying about getting married?" I said. "And you know you said you wouldn't want to, unless there was some sort of a slip-up?"

"Yeah?" Ann said.

"Well, if there was a slip-up, you wouldn't do the other thing, would you?"

Ann sat up.

"What other thing?" she said.

"You know," I said. "Over to England on the boat and back, and no trouble."

Maybe that was what Mike was here for. Maybe he was taking Rose back with him. But she wouldn't. Rose would never do a thing like that to a child that was in her.

"Oh," Ann said, sounding embarrassed. "You mean, get rid of the baby."

"Yes, *that*," I said.

Then she looked at me.

"*You're* not, are you?" she said, directly.

"What?"

"You've not got yourself pregnant, Kathleen?" she asked.

"Blethers," I said.

"You're not, are you?" she persisted.

"Indeed and I am not!" I said.

"You had me going for a minute there," Ann said.

We were both sitting up now. Imelda was wandering along the hedge, with her hair dark against the yellow whin blossom.

"You would know how to tell…?"

I felt myself going crimson.

"I wasn't born yesterday, you know," I told her.

"Sorry," she said. "Only if you were, you know, in trouble or something, I'd want to help."

How could she think I was so stupid that I'd let that happen to me? Just because I don't talk like her or read books. I could have told her I keep myself to myself, and time enough for that when the time came.

"Nobody is doing that to me, yet a while," I told her, and immediately all that was in my mind was that *somebody* had done it to Rose. It may sound daft, but up to that I'd just been thinking about Rose, not the other somebody who was in it.

"Good," Ann said. "But there's no need to sound so grim about it. Wait until you meet someone you fancy."

"I'm off the idea just now, thank you," I said.

"Another Teresa!" she said.

"There's nothing wrong with Teresa."

"Nothing that a bit of fun wouldn't put right," Ann said. "Thirty-something, and never been kissed."

Now that she'd stopped thinking I was pregnant there was a change in her. I never heard her talk that way before.

"You never … you never did it, did you?" I said.

Imelda had her skirt tucked up in her pants. She had her back to us, and she was ducked down poking at a hole in the hedge.

"Not yet," she said. "But here's hoping!"

"I mightn't *ever* do it," I said.

"What about your hunky prince?" she said.

"You know you will. Everybody does. There's nothing so awful about it."

Then Imelda let a whoop out of her, and next moment Frank came over the hedge and scooped her up in his arms. He carried her up the field, towards us, the shape of him picked out against the whins, and the blue of the lake in the distance.

"You talk decent now," I told Ann. "You talk decent. None of that chat in front of Frank."

"Don't fancy him, myself," she said, skittishly.

"You're too late, anyroad," I said. "Frank's made his bed."

I couldn't imagine Frank like that, and Carmel. And Rose – Rose and *who*?

"Just the girls I'm looking for," Frank said, and he had us off to the bottom of the field, to fix the gap in the hedge, Imelda and all.

"If that child pokes her eye out on the hedge you'll have Carmel to answer to," I told him.

When we had the job done, we went to the house for a cup of tea. Mammy had one with us. She'd decided she was having a bad day with the leg, so she was stopping in her chair.

Ann hopped in where a wiser one would have held her peace.

"Is your leg sore, Mrs Fay?" she said, all innocent.

"Divil the bit," said Mammy.

"Did you have the doctor?" Ann asked, being polite and concerned the Belfast way her-Mammy-the-teacher had taught her.

"Cow's piss on the doctor!" Mammy said.

55

Ann's face was a sight!

"Do you not like doctors, Mrs Fay?" Ann asked, after a minute.

"No," said Mammy, suddenly catching on that it wasn't one of her own she was talking to. If it had been me or Rose or Teresa we would have known all about it, if we had asked the question.

"I've no time for doctors," Mammy told her. "They'd saw the leg off you as soon as look at you."

"What did I do?" Ann asked me, when we were back out in the yard.

"She doesn't like Dr Mallon," I said.

"Why?"

"She blames him for putting Daddy in hospital," I said. "Dr Mallon put him when he didn't want to go. He was eight months lying there in the Daisy Hill, and that is why Mammy doesn't like the man."

"If old Mr Fay was sick…?" Ann said.

"She wanted him here," I said. "Daddy wanted to be here too, so he'd die in his own place, with his own ones. But Mallon laid on that he would be better in hospital, and maybe coming home one day on his own two feet. So that's how he died down in the Daisy Hill in Newry, and Mammy not near him when he went. So there you are."

"But that's years ago," Ann said. "Years and years. And he was an old man, he was going to die anyway."

"I don't care how old he was," I said. "That's

got nothing to do with it."

"I suppose old people think like that," Ann said.

"It is just yesterday to Mammy," I said.

"What age is she?" Ann asked.

"Old enough," I said. I'm never sure what age Mammy is, for she is close about it. "She's as good as any man about the place, on her good days," I said. "Frank would tell you that."

"Frank is the eldest?" Ann asked.

"Frank is near forty," I said. "Teresa is next. Then Rose, and our Mike, and our Bernie that died, and then a long, long road, and there's me."

"Y-e-s," Ann said, giving me a look. I thought for a minute she was going to say something else – maybe she did know about Rose's baby after all. Mary O'Connor must have told her, or she'd spotted Rose's tummy. Whatever it was she was thinking to say, she didn't say it.

"It's all no ad for family planning," was what she came up with.

"We wouldn't have *those* things about the place," I told her.

Then I wondered about Carmel. Carmel only has one child, and her four years married. Frank would never let her use those things, Frank wouldn't. Carmel not having another baby is just God's will.

With a few more kids, Carmel would have to get rid of the fine furniture, and it would stop her high jinks going into Dundalk. I didn't say to Ann about Frank and Carmel, because it was none of her business. Ann would probably say Carmel would be just right to use those things.

That's a sin.

Anybody round here would tell you that is a sin, but not as big a sin as the other. There's nothing worse than the other – killing a child that's in your body and one of God's creatures with a soul of its own.

"Would you take that child of Carmel's up the stairs and wet her face!" Mammy shouted from the house.

"I'll see you then," Ann said, and she went off.

I went up to the bathroom with Imelda.

Mammy had been feeding her sugar again, and the stuff was sticking round her mouth.

Mike was just coming out of the bathroom, bleary-eyed.

"Just getting up," he said, and he took a dig at Imelda with his finger. She shied off.

"Don't scare the child, Mike," I said.

"She's not scared of her own uncle!" Mike said.

"Away and make yourself decent," I said, for he was in his vest, and all black and scraggy round his chin. "You're a lie-a-bed."

"I need my beauty sleep," he said.

"Do you not get up early for your work?" I said, thinking all the building ones I know have to be off early.

"The work's a bit iffy-butty these days," Mike said.

"Is that what brought you home?" I said, for I'd

been wondering. "Free board and lodging?"

"You're too smart!" he said, and he laughed. "Watch out, or I'll take you away with me, when I go."

"Would you?" I said, wondering if he meant it – and if I'd want to go, if he did.

"For a holiday?" he said.

"No. No, if I was left school, and everything, and I wanted away..."

He quietened down. "We'll have a talk about that some time, Kathleen," he said. "What put that in your head anyway?"

"You gave me a *travelling* clock," I said. "I thought maybe it was a hint."

"Aye. Maybe it was, now. Maybe it was," he said.

I went in to Imelda, who was half drowning herself with the tap.

What had put it into my head just then to ask about going away? I *knew* the clock was meant to suggest it – that's the sort of thing Mike thinks is very clever, I could see through it all right. But going away...

I suppose it was the upset over Rose that put it in my head.

When Rose had her baby, there would be changes. Maybe it was a time for changes.

I could do what Ann said, and go to Belfast where she'd show me things, and I might be a teacher even, if I was smart enough. Or Mike could take me, then it would be London, and high times

– or maybe I'd off on my own somewhere, to Dublin maybe, where I'd not be so far from home – though it would be far enough – or to Belfast, with the heathen Protestants.

Stay home and be another Rose or Teresa, or take to the high road, like Mike?

"Come on here, till I splatter your face, Imelda, baby," I told her, and I gave her a big hug and stuck the sponge on her nose.

CHAPTER SEVEN

Mammy ordered me off to town with Frank for the shopping, with a list of dos and don'ts as long as your arm. You'd think I'd never done it before. Probably she was only fussing me to keep her mind off Rose. Frank dropped me off at O'Hanlon's shop, and he went on into Broganstown for the milk money from the Co-op.

I got the stuff from O'Hanlon's all packed in my bag and paid for, and then I stood out on the road and thumbed it, because I didn't fancy lugging the stuff back.

Who should I get but big Brendan Regan! He's not the Regans in our lane, he's the Regans from the houses outside town on the Broganstown side. When he saw it was me with the bag he turned the car round and said he would run me out.

I settled back in the car, front seat. He had the back seat filled with blocks.

"How's old Mrs Fay?" he said.

61

"Fine," I said.

"And Frank? Frank's the boy."

"Frank's fine," I said.

"And the Micky one?"

"He's home," I said.

"Where was he?"

"London."

"At the building?"

"He was," I said. I didn't want to let on Mike was out of a job again.

"Old Tom Walsh seen him with your Carmel," he said. "Her and Frank."

"That's right," I said.

"And the women?" he said. "Rose and Teresa?"

If he was hoping I'd let something slip about Rose, he had no hope.

"Doing fine," I said, never letting on. But he'd likely know. They would all likely know by this time. You can't keep a thing like that quiet round Kiltarragh, or the townlands.

"And yourself?" he said.

"I'm dandy," I said.

"You're getting to be a big girl," he said.

I didn't say a thing.

"You go down the parish hall?" he said. "To the hops?"

Nobody calls dances "hops" any more. We have the canon's discos two nights in the week, down in the hall, when the bingo isn't on.

"I go the odd time," I said. "I'm not fussed."

"Peter Walsh was asking," he said.

Was he? It was news to me, but I never let on.

"He didn't see you down there," Brendan said. "You'll maybe go down now your Mike is back?"

"I might," I said.

"I'll tell Peter he might see you there," Brendan said, and he let me off at the foot of the lane. He didn't go up our lane because he knows about the bumps and his exhaust-pipe is held on with a prayer.

I lugged the bag up the lane.

Peter Walsh!

Peter Walsh for my hunky prince? No way!

Mrs Regan was out at the front, spying as usual. She's so sharp at it she'll cut herself one day.

"Was that Begley's car you were in?" she said.

"No," I said, letting on I wasn't all ears, but I was. What Begleys did she mean? The only Begleys I knew of were the Begleys at Killeep, and I don't know them to speak to. But if she was saying it, she was saying it to get a reaction out of me. The Renault up the lane must have been somebody Begley then, and it didn't need my Sherlock Holmes hat for me to figure out what that meant.

Rose and one of the Begleys.

The Begleys have a bit of land, and there's a cousin does the scrap and old cars, you can see the sun wink on them on the Scarratstown Road.

"I just thought it might be Begley's car," she said.

"Brendan Regan gave me a lift," I said.

That soured her.

The Regans from our lane don't sort with the

Regans from the town. Brendan Regan took his Uncle Patsy's mountain off him three lettings ago, and now Patsy has the cattle away down the townland, and he's not pleased. Our Frank had his eye on Regan's mountain at the same time, but Mammy told him to keep out of the bidding, for the Regans are our neighbours. Frank says we should have gone for it, but Mammy has the purse strings and the say so. So we didn't get Patsy Regan's mountain.

"How's Rose keeping?" Mrs Regan called after me.

I never let on that I'd heard.

I could have cut her throat for her, cheerfully!

Rose and one of the Begleys! If he'd come up to our house to see Mammy, he was owning up to it and doing the decent thing anyroad. Maybe he'd marry her and then, if Carmel got the new house she was on about, Rose and her Begley could move into Carmel's and we'd all still be together. I didn't want Rose to be away from Kiltarragh.

It would be all right for Rose, if he was nice. He'd have to be nice, wouldn't he, or she'd not have...

I just switched off about that, for I didn't want to think about it. I came round the dip thinking about Peter Walsh, and was he asking after me or was Brendan Regan only pulling my leg? Mind you, I wasn't sure I wanted anyone asking after me, ever, after what had happened to Rose.

I came up the dip by the barn and past Carmel's

and into our yard, up to our house – and there was a hole in it!

Mammy was out in the yard on a kitchen chair, and there was a hole in the wall, right up by the roof, and our Mike's head sticking out of it.

"My window!" I said.

"That's right," he said. "You'll have a fine view tonight, Kathleen."

I would have, if he'd got the stuff first. Trust Mike to knock a hole in the wall, and *then* go off for the glass and timber. He tried all round, but Sorleys was stock-taking, and he couldn't get what he wanted.

That left me with a fine open air bedroom for the night.

Frank took a look at it when he came back, and then he gave Mike hell, and then he got an old tarpaulin from the hedge and fixed it up, but he wasn't too pleased.

"My little brother is only off the boat from England, and he has the house knocked down," Frank said.

"He was making me my window," I said.

"I would have made you your window, one of these days," Frank said.

It was on the tip of my tongue to tell him he would have, if Carmel hadn't kept him so busy, but I didn't.

They decided I was to go in the big bed with Mammy for the night, because my room was bust up. Then Mammy changed her mind and talked to

Frank about it, and Frank said I was to go down the lane to Carmel's for the night.

You should have seen Carmel's face!

She wasn't too pleased, but Frank said his piece, and there was nothing she could do about it.

I had my tea up at our house and then I got the buckets and helped Frank with the feed, traipsing across the fields. He was grumbling about Mike, but I kept my mouth shut, though a part of me was grumbling as well. I'd been wanting the window, but at the same time I wanted my own room. Maybe it was just that I was upset, I didn't want to be in a stranger's house with Carmel. Frank is no stranger, but Carmel is. She chose to be that way. We didn't make her. We got the cows in, and fed, and then I stuck my nightie in a bag and went down the lane to Carmel's. I took my bedspread with me wishing I could curl up under it in the barn or somewhere, anywhere but Carmel's house.

"Your lodger's come, Carmel," I called out, standing by the door. I wouldn't walk in on her like I would on our ones.

"Come in and make comfy," Carmel said.

She had biscuits and a cup of tea all ready and laid out for me, which isn't like Carmel. I reckoned Frank had given her a mouthful and she was trying to butter me up, to please him.

Imelda came wandering out of the bedroom when she heard my voice, wanting a Starry Night story.

"You'll get no such thing," Carmel said.

"Never mind, Carmel," I said, for I thought I'd be glad to be with the child and out of range of Carmel's conversation. "Don't be hard on the child. I'll tell her a story."

"You Fays have her spoiled," Carmel said. "Telling her stories to all hours, and stuffing sweeties into her."

She'd found out about Mike's sweeties.

That was my fault.

I'd had Imelda on my knee on the sofa the night before, when she was whining, and the sticky stuff on her hands had got onto the posh sofa. Rose was going to sponge it off before Carmel and Frank got back, but she must have forgotten.

"I don't like sticking to my furniture," Carmel said, and she shut Imelda back in her room, and paid no heed to her whinges.

Instead, Carmel laid into me about child rearing and what was right for Imelda, and what wasn't. It was all fine, except that she left me to do the baby-chasing three days a week while she was in Dundalk earning good money.

"I'm very sorry if you're put out, Carmel," I said, letting her know fine well that I wasn't. "Maybe if I'm no good at looking after the child you should come home and take a hand yourself."

That got her!

"What would we do for money?" she said, beginning to heat up. "You don't think Frank pays for all this, do you?"

"Nobody has ever gone short at Fays'," I said.

"The farm is a good living."

"Aye!" she said. "Aye. On Frank's back, it is! One thing I do know, and I'll give it to you straight. Frank is not taking on any more responsibility than he has already. Them that reaps can sow."

She went off to her bed.

She was on about Rose.

Well, we'd see about that. If the Begley one didn't marry Rose, we'd see what would happen. Our Frank would never turn Rose from the door. The Fays stick together. That I know.

Or I thought I knew.

Suppose it was me? Suppose I was Rose? What would I do? Suppose she didn't even *want* to marry this Begley? What would Rose do?

I had the feeling, inside me, that the whole thing was going to be a terrible mess. And there was another feeling, something that came at me when I was sitting in Carmel's watching her TV with the sound down low, so I wouldn't wake her.

I had the feeling something *else* was up, something I hadn't got to grips with. I worried at it like a dog with a flea, and the more I circled round it, the more I came back to Ann and the way she always seemed to be stopping herself from saying something about our family and then she didn't say what it was. How could Ann know something about us that I didn't? And if she knew something, why didn't she up and tell me?

We were supposed to be friends.

The only answer to that one was to get hold of

Ann and have it out with her.

I sat there, long after the TV was off, wondering if I had the nerve to do it.

CHAPTER EIGHT

I was up early in the morning off Carmel's sofa, and up to our house where I peeled the spuds and got Mammy's leg done, and then I set my face to it, and headed over to O'Connor's.

If Ann knew anything I didn't, she could just tell me. I'm big enough to know where babies come from.

Big deal!

Ann wasn't about. James O'Connor had taken her off to Dundalk for the day, so I was left with all my fretting for nothing.

"How is Rose?" Mary O'Connor asked me.

She looked me straight in the eye. I think she knew I knew, but she didn't like to say anything straight out.

I didn't bat an eyelid. I wasn't going to give her the satisfaction – no, perhaps that's not fair. Mary O'Connor is an old talker, but she's not like Mrs Regan. I knew Mary would help Rose, if she could.

"Rose is fine," I said.

"And yourself?" she said.

"I'm fine," I said.

She didn't say anything for a minute, and then she said: "You know, Kathleen, any time you want to come across here, you're welcome. We're not like some round here. We'd not hold anything against you."

"I know that, Mrs O'Connor," I said.

"That's what neighbours are for," she said. "Whatever talk there is, the Fays hold their heads high as far as we're concerned."

"That's very good of you, Mrs O'Connor," I said, but I could feel the heart going down me, into my boots.

"You've friends here," she said. "You particularly, Kathleen."

I went away.

She was a decent woman. She was trying to say she'd give me any help she could – only I wasn't the one that needed help, was I? It was Rose needed helping.

I put it out of my head. She was only saying she wouldn't spread any old gossip about the Fays, like any decent neighbour would. There's talk and there's talk but you don't talk to strangers about your own ones. There's just things you don't say though you know about them well enough. Mary O'Connor wouldn't carry Rose's tale with her. Mind you, it would be hard for Mary O'Connor

71

not to be in the middle when there was gossip going on, that's for sure.

Why was she saying me, *particularly*?

When I got back to the house Mike was bouncing round the yard with a trailer full of window, and a help mate – Peter Walsh!

"Hi, Kathleen," Peter said, but I went straight on inside. I was in no mood for Peter Walsh. Peter's twenty-one, he'd have the key of the door if the Walshes had a door to call their own, which they haven't. The Walshes haven't two pennies to rub together.

So much for my hunky prince!

Peter and Mike got ladders against the side of the house, and Mike went up them. When he came down he wasn't too pleased. I stayed out of the way, but I caught the gist of it through the window.

"We need another foot on her, Peter," he said, and he went to get the sledgehammer from the barn.

Mammy brought Peter Walsh into the kitchen.

"Make this man a cup of tea, Kathleen," she said. "He's only bringing you your window."

Peter sat down at the table and perspired at me. He had a beer gut on him. He was all red in his woolly hat and his dungarees. His hair came out from beneath the hat, and curled up round his ears. He had big round hands with broken nails. I didn't fancy my beau – if he *was* my beau.

"Are you in work, Peter?" Mammy asked.

"Down Lundy's houses," he said.

Lundy is a big builder round our way, but not as big as James O'Connor.

"Did our Mike get the window off Lundy?" Mammy asked.

"He did and he didn't," said Peter, with a wink. Then he added: "Lundy has a part share of more houses round these parts than he knows of."

Mammy didn't look too pleased.

"It's all in the game!" Peter said, grinning at her with his dirty teeth.

"You're a decent man to give Mike a hand," Mammy said.

Peter sat there, gawking at me. Every so often he would give me a wink, but he didn't say anything, and I didn't say anything back. I was dang sure I wasn't going near the canon's disco till he lost the notion – if ever he had it.

Mike started banging on the wall, and all the cups did a dance.

They put Peter's car in against the house, with a tarpaulin on it, and then they got up on top and started beating hell out of the wall. It was a good thing the car was a wreck off some scrap-heap, because the stone was raining down on it. I took Imelda out to watch, though we stayed over the far side of the yard, by the barn, where we wouldn't get hurt.

They were going like the clappers when Frank came storming into the yard.

"What the hell are you at?" Frank demanded.

73

"Fitting the window," said Mike, all cheerful. He had his shirt off, and the sun was glittering on his back.

"Look to the roof!" Frank shouted.

We all looked.

Some of the old rafters must have parted. There was a split up the tiles, and a sort of dip at the top, and a big crack up the end of the house.

"You've done the gable!" Frank said, sounding real mad at Mike.

I took a look round the side of the house, with Imelda, and right enough he had. There was a jagged crack right up the gable.

"That'll take some fixing!" Frank said.

Mike hopped down off the car roof and took a look at the gable.

"How did that happen?" he said.

"Some London cowboy took a sledgehammer to the house," said Frank. "That's how it happened. And fine well you know how it happened. Could you not let well alone?"

Peter Walsh, clever enough, summed it up that there would be no more wall breaking that day. He came down to the ground and took off his woolly hat, which he scrunched up and stuck in his belt.

"I'd better be getting back, Mrs Fay," he said to Mammy, and he whipped the tarpaulin off the car, sending stones and rubble spilling round the yard, and hopped into the driving seat and drove off down the lane, bump-bump-bump along the rocks – my hunky prince!

Mike and Frank were round the gable end, yelling at each other.

"Take the child out of this, Kathleen," Mammy said.

I took Imelda down the lane out of earshot.

Rose and Teresa were coming up it, with their bags.

"The soap is shut," Rose said. "We're back on holidays."

Her tummy was really big, beneath her floppy coat. How could I not have noticed it?

"Aye, well," I said. "Don't go up there. Mike has half the wall down and the roof is gone and Frank is giving him hell and Mammy is after the pair of them and I don't know what will come of it."

We listened, and we could hear the swearing down the lane.

"No job, no money, and now no house!" said Teresa, with a long face.

"It's dang funny!" said Rose, suddenly, and she started laughing. That set me off. I don't know what was funny about it, with them having to go back on the dole and the house knocked down, but it was funny. Rose and I got the giggles, but Teresa never said a word. Her face set like concrete.

"D'you hear him?" wailed Rose. "Would you listen to Frank!"

"Wait'll he has to tell Carmel," I said.

"She'll destroy him!" giggled Rose.

"Mind the child," said Teresa, taking hold of

Imelda. Imelda was gawping at us.

Then there was a clatter in the lane and Frank's old car came out from behind our barn, and headed down past us, with Mike at the wheel. He gave us a toot on the horn, but he didn't stop.

Silence.

"Hold on here, you pair, till I spy out the land," Rose said, and she went on up the lane towards the house.

"I'm glad you think the whole thing is funny," said Teresa, watching her go.

"It's not, but it *is*," I said.

"God, but you're like *her*," Teresa said, bitterly.

"Who?"

"The Kiltarragh bicycle," Teresa said.

"What?" I said, still in half a giggle.

"Oh, you can laugh," Teresa said. "You don't know the half of what I have to put up with."

"How d'you mean?" I said, with the laugh dying in me. There was a glisten in Teresa's eye. She was really upset.

She set her mouth, and didn't reply.

"What's all this about a bicycle?" I said.

"That's what they're calling her," Teresa said.

"Calling who?" I said.

"Rose," she said.

Then I understood. It fairly stopped me in my tracks.

"See you keep yourself to yourself," Teresa said. "They'll be thinking we're all the same up here. All like her. I tell you this, Kathleen, if you start taking after her and her ways you can clear off this place."

She went on up the lane, banging her bag against her leg. Then she stopped, and turned.

"Don't you let that Peter Walsh one touch you," she said. Then she scooped Imelda up in her arms, and went on.

I was a long time going back up the lane, but when I got there Frank was sitting on the yard wall looking at the house, with a cup of tea in his hand.

Mike's hole in the wall had split right down to the lintel above the door.

"He's a mad git, that brother of mine!" Frank said, supping his tea. "I'll need to take the whole wall down there, and build her up again."

"He meant well," I said, thinking that all Mike was trying to do was to fix my window.

"Don't *you* start, Kathleen," Frank said, and he gestured towards the house. "To hear Mammy you'd think it was time we had home improvements and Mike was only speeding things up a bit."

And he went off down the yard.

I went into the house.

Mammy was by the range. She had taken down the photograph of Daddy from the shelf. It was the one in his British army uniform, with Seamus Grillen and Hugh Meaghan, when they were in Tobruk with the Brits against Hitler.

"Our Mike has a likeness of him," Mammy said, lowering herself down into her chair, with the photograph on her lap.

She'd gone all moody.

I don't like that photograph. Daddy has short hair in it, and he's a bit like an older Mike, but he's dressed up like a Brit. I can't get over the ones from round here fighting in the Brit's army.

I put the photograph back up on the shelf, beside the one of me and Mammy and Rose and Teresa and Frank and Mike. You wouldn't know it was me, because I'm the one in the robe, just after getting christened. If you were looking for me, you'd think I was Rose or Teresa. They must have been about the age I am now, when it was getting taken. Only you'd know it wasn't me, because of the black hair. Teresa had a fine head of hair on her then, but now she has it all cut. Rose's hair was just the same, but you can't see it in the photo because she has a hat on.

The Kiltarragh bicycle!

I know what that meant well enough. It was an awful thing to call her, and just like those ones down at the soap. They'd be saying we were all the same – only I'd be a wee one, a tricycle.

If the same Peter Walsh thought all he had to do was take me up a lane, he had another think coming.

"Mike made a mess of the wall," I said to Mammy.

"Frank'll sort things out," Mammy said.

Frank this and Frank that, but when it came to who was her apple pie, that was the other fella. I could *hurt* for Frank sometimes, listening to

Mammy praising Mike, and worrying about him being away, and wanting him back, and going on about what he'd do about the place, when the truth is Mike walked out on us, years ago.

Mike gone, Frank married, Rose in trouble... Teresa was the one who stayed put, looking out for everybody but herself. Ann was right. Great nun material! It was a shame. Why couldn't someone say to her that she'd a right to her own life? I suppose it's just that sort of personal, private thing nobody here says out loud, though everybody knows it.

"Would you get Imelda her tea, Kathleen?" Mammy said.

"Yes, Mammy," I said.

"And put something by for our cowboy, when he gets back," she said, meaning Mike.

"Yes, Mammy," I repeated.

Oh she'd look out for Mike, all right. But not poor Frank. Maybe Carmel was right after all, and Mammy just had Frank as a dogsbody.

"I'm off upstairs for a lie down," Mammy said, and she clumped off up the stairs, leaving me in the kitchen.

A maid-of-all-work!

All Mammy wanted was Frank and Rose and Teresa and me, tied round her, so we couldn't move – and Mike, if she could get him, but she couldn't, because he'd got out of the way, on his travels.

"You're just selfish!" I felt like telling her.

"You're a selfish old thing."

A part of me thought it was true, and another part didn't like it. How could I think a thing like that about her, my own mammy?

CHAPTER NINE

That evening, Frank went over to O'Connor's house, and he had James back with him. Ann came across as well.

James took a look at the hole in our house. Then Frank got the ladder, and he and James went up on the roof.

Rose and Teresa and Mammy and all were out in the yard looking at them.

James O'Connor got a hand hammer and a spike, and prised at one of the rafters in our roof. It split across.

"There you are, Frank!" he said.

Frank came down off the roof, and James came after him.

"A good wind would blow her off, Frank," James said. "The timber's rotted. You've more problems than the gap in your wall."

"It's a fine roof," Mammy said, but nobody paid any attention to her.

81

James and Frank went back across the fields to O'Connor's house, and Ann and Imelda and I tagged along behind them.

When we got into O'Connor's, James O'Connor got out the whiskey, and the two of them went into James's business rooms and had a long talk.

"What's happening?" Ann asked me.

We were watching *Coronation Street* with Imelda.

"Our house is falling down," I said.

"I know that," she said.

"Frank told Mammy he would get James across to see what it would cost to fix it," I said.

"I thought your brothers would do that between them," Ann said. "They do most things, don't they?"

"Frank does," I said. "You couldn't count on Mike."

"Well, Frank then," said Ann.

"Frank's no builder," I said. "He was telling Mammy he *thought* he might manage it himself, but he'd need to have a word with James first, before he'd try it. He was hoping James could lend him a tradesman, and he'd do the labouring himself."

"I see," said Ann.

"Only we didn't know the roof was rotten," I said. Mind you, we had a good idea. It's been letting the rain in for years, and bits are always flying off of it.

"What'll you do?" Ann said.

"Me?" I said. "Nothing. Frank will fix something with James. Frank's the man about the place."

"It isn't Frank's house," Ann said.

"Of course it is," I said, not seeing what she was getting at.

"Mrs Fay owns it," said Ann.

"But it's all down to Frank," I said.

"What about Rose and Teresa?" Ann said. "Don't they have a say?"

"Why would they?"

"Well, it is as much their house as it is Frank's," Ann said.

"No it isn't," I said.

"But…"

"Frank runs it."

"What about Mike?" said Ann. "If old Mrs Fay died, wouldn't he want his share?"

"Mike wouldn't live here if you paid him," I said.

"He's still entitled to his share if you sell the house," Ann said.

"We *can't* sell the house," I said, spelling it out for her. "The house and the land walk together, and Mammy has them all, and when Mammy dies, Frank will get it."

"I only hope she's made a will," said Ann.

Maybe Ann had something. If Mammy died, and Frank got the place, that would be the same as giving it to Carmel. I couldn't see Rose and Teresa taking kindly to Carmel ruling the roost.

I never thought of it like that, with Mammy dying. Carmel would be in our house, bossing us around. Frank would never let her, would he? She has him turned soft in the head, that Carmel one. What right would she have to come in over our heads, taking the roof from over us? What roof there was left, that is.

Ann had me worried by the time Frank came out, looking worried himself. He chucked Imelda up on his shoulders, and we started back down by the lake.

"It's a bad do, Kathleen," he said, shaking his head.

We were down by Daddy's rock, and he'd put Imelda on it, to rest himself. "A bad do, altogether."

"Can James O'Connor not fix it?" I asked.

"Fix it!" said Frank, sounding disgusted. He sat down. I was up on the rock, beside Imelda. I saw a thing I never saw before. I could see Frank's scalp through his hair. He was going baldy.

"He could fix it," Frank said. "But the way James O'Connor has it, the fixing wouldn't be worth the candle."

"What?" I said.

"Money," he said.

"Would we not get grants?" I said. Everybody round here gets grants from the Brits and the EEC. That's how James O'Connor and the Lundys make their money, building things on grants.

"Not the way the house is," said Frank. "The drains are wrong, and the walls are wrong, and the floor is wrong, and the kitchen is wrong and there is nothing about the place that the grant inspectors wouldn't want fixing before they'd give us our money."

"Could we not get a grant for a brand new bungalow, like James O'Connor builds for other people?" I said. "James O'Connor would know how to work it. Then we could have a walk-through kitchen and big windows like the O'Connors have."

I thought it would be great. Maybe Mike was right to take a hammer to our house.

"You'd like that, wouldn't you, our Kathleen?" he said.

"You're to build me a room of my own," I said. "A proper room, with windows, and electric points, and a carpet. And there's to be a shower you can wear a plastic hat in, like the O'Connors."

"O'Connors this, O'Connors that. You know you, Kathleen?" he said. "You've been listening to your own stories too long, like the tales you tell Imelda. Starry Nights! You're to be a princess in a new bungalow, with young Peter Walsh a prince coming up the lane, to carry you off in your plastic hat?"

"I'd not let Peter Walsh over the step!" I said. "I'm having no Peter Walsh clumping round my new house in his boots."

Frank stood up and stretched himself.

"Is that what you'll do, Frank?" I asked, hoping

that it was, because I could fancy myself in a new bungalow. Maybe Mammy would let me have a television for myself. I could get a little one, for my new room, and then I would lie in bed and watch it like the dames in *Dallas*.

"A house for Mammy," he said.

"A bungalow, Frank," I said. "A bungalow with no stairs, for she has a time of it going up them with her leg. It wouldn't cost us a penny, with the grants." I kept on at him as we walked up the field, seeking to encourage him, for I didn't want him put off my Starry Night house, when I almost had it.

"You get nothing for nothing, Kathleen," he said. "When we do it, James O'Connor will have a fine screw out of my pocket, and you know he will."

When ... so he was going to do it!

"Build us a big one," I said. "Build a big one with rooms out the back, and you can quit renting the house down the lane and all move in with us in Mammy's new house, you and Carmel and Imelda."

Frank raised an eyebrow, but he didn't say a word.

We went up into the yard, and Frank went to the house to talk to Mammy.

"We're getting a brand new house," I told Rose.

"Your leg!" said Rose, but she had to believe me when I told her all about it.

"Good has come out of it, anyway," Teresa

said, when Rose told her. The three of us sat on the wall, looking at the old house and trying to see the new one, with the windows and the shower, and the plastic hats.

"A red shower hat for Teresa," I said. "A blue one for me, a wee tiny pink one for Imelda and a hat with roses on it for Rose."

"It would take more than a shower hat to fix me," Rose said. It was funny the way she said it. It didn't sound like Rose at all.

Teresa put her hand over Rose's.

It was the oddest ever. There they were, sitting on the yard wall, holding hands like wee girls – and a few hours before Teresa had been calling her dirty names, down our lane.

Maybe Rose wouldn't even be there to see the new house. She might be away, living somewhere else, with her new baby.

"Blethers!" I said. I wasn't going to let anything get in the way of the biggest Starry Night we'd ever had.

A brand new house on the hill at Kiltarragh, with big windows looking out over the lake, and all of us living in it as if we were kings and queens and princesses.

Imelda was playing round the yard.

"Take the child down to Carmel's, Kathleen," Teresa said softly, and I did it, leaving Rose and Teresa sitting on the wall.

They were just like the two in my christening photograph, only fifteen years on. Two twigs on

87

the one branch, but they didn't sort. Usually, they didn't. But when it mattered, like now, when Rose was really hurting, then Teresa'd go to her. They had all their past to hold them together. When I got back from Carmel's they'd gone down by the lake, to the rock.

Teresa had her brown skirt on, and Rose was in a yellow one, and the colours picked them out against the blue of the lake and the grey of the rocks.

They were talking.

They'd be talking about Rose's baby, and what to do about it.

CHAPTER TEN

I was sleeping under my bedspread on Carmel's green sofa when the telephone went. I got up and answered it.

"Is that Fay's?" said a man's voice.

"Yes."

"Could I speak to Francis Fay, please?" said the voice.

Who'd be calling Frank, *Francis*? Francis *is* his name, but everybody calls him Frank.

"Who is it?" I said.

"Scarratstown RUC," he said.

"Oh gee!" I said, and then Frank came out of the bedroom in his pyjamas.

"It's the police, Frank!" I said.

"Bleeding blazes!" Frank said, and he grabbed the telephone off me.

Carmel came out into the lounge, wrapping her frilly dressing gown round her.

"It's the police, Carmel," I said. "It must be

89

our Mike."

"Wheest!" Carmel said, signing me to shut up.

The police! The police and *Mike*. It had to be Mike. They'd have him beaten to a pulp, like the time they took Patsy Regan.

"Maybe it's the army picked him up," I said to Carmel. "Him not knowing his way about like he used to. Maybe he went where he shouldn't."

Carmel put her hand over my mouth.

Frank was yes-ing, and no-ing, and that's right-ing, then he came off the telephone, and stood looking at us.

"They got him!" he said. "The Mike one."

"Oh, Frank," Carmel said. "Oh Frank, love."

"Is he all right?" I said. "Did they beat him, Frank?"

"He's right as rain, by all accounts," Frank said, moving back towards the bedroom. "Where's me trousers, Carmel?"

"Is it … is he mixed up with the IRA?" I said. "Blowing things up?"

"Him?" said Frank, contemptuously. "Not him!"

Then he said something to Carmel that I didn't catch.

"He didn't, Frank!" she said.

"Oh, but he did. Playing the smart man, back from the big city, paying off all our scores," Frank said, and he went into the bedroom.

"What is it, Carmel?" I said. If he was all right, and it wasn't the boys, the IRA, then what was it?

90

"My sweet brother-in-law is sleeping it off in a cell in Scarratstown," said Carmel.

"And Guess Who has to get in the car and go down to fetch him out!" said Frank, bitterly. He came out of the bedroom, stuffing his shirt inside his trousers, and hooked his coat off the chair.

"Keys, Carmel?" he said.

Carmel went to the desk and came back with the keys of her Mini. I knew they were Carmel's keys, because she has a St Christopher key tag, and a holy medal on them.

"God bless," she said.

He went out into the yard, and a minute or two later he had the engine going, and off he went with his headlights cutting into the yellow of the whins down the lane.

We were both stood at the door.

"Come on in," Carmel said, pulling the frills round her. "There's no prizes for freezing."

We went back in.

"Put the kettle on, Kathleen," Carmel said.

I did it.

"What did he do, Carmel?" I said. "What did our Mike do?"

"Oh, the bottle talked," she said.

Mike likes a drink, true enough, but he's not like Patsy Regan. Or he *wasn't*, anyway. Maybe he'd got more of a taste for it, away in England, with things not going right for him there.

"What did he do, Carmel?" I repeated.

"He got in a fight with some people," said Carmel.

91

"Who? What people?"

"Frank will tell you all about it when he gets back with the prodigal brother," Carmel said.

The kettle boiled, and I made the tea. When I came back in Carmel had the blankets off the sofa, and folded. She was sitting there. She'd got a cigarette from somewhere.

I didn't know she smoked.

"I didn't know you smoked," I told her.

"I have my moments," she said, and she gave a kind of dry laugh.

"Does Frank know you smoke?" I said, thinking of the pay Frank gave out to Rose, when he caught her at it.

"Frank's not my boss."

"He won't like it."

"Then he can go hump himself, and his whole family!" Carmel said, sounding as if she was wild.

"That's no way to talk," I said, affronted at her using language like that about our Frank.

"Frank this and Frank that!" she said. "That's all there is from up the house all day, and small thanks Frank gets for it."

"Well, I don't know at all, Carmel," I said, sounding as put out as I was.

"No, you don't," she said. "But you will one day if you go off and get married and find you've not married a man but a houseboy, at the beck and call of a pack of women."

"Indeed, that's not so," I said. "Frank's his own man."

"Tell that to the marines," she said.

I gave her her tea.

"There's buns in the kitchen, if you'd like one," she said.

"No thanks," I said.

We sat there, both of us feeling a bit daft. I was afraid to say anything in case it got worse, when I couldn't really see what was getting at her anyway. Mike, I suppose, and being woken up in the middle of the night for Frank to go down to the police station.

I sat there looking at the Sacred Heart up above the fireplace. Carmel's auntie gave it to her for the wedding. It has a dandy frame.

"I'm not getting at you, pet," Carmel said. "But there's some things that go on that you'll understand better when you're older."

Oh great, I thought, *just like school*.

She stubbed out the cigarette, though it was only half smoked.

"The thing is, Kathleen, you marry someone, and you have a picture in your mind of the way it'll be, d'you know? Like there'll be you, and your man, and your house, and the child..."

"Imelda is a grand girl," I said.

"And Frank is a fine man," she said. "But all this!"

"All what?" I said, looking round me, too. Quinn's is not a bad house, and they'd spent a fortune on the furniture, though they'd got it HP from some man James O'Connor knew down in Keady.

"All these … *complications*," she said.

"What complications?"

"I want a place of my own, Kathleen. I want a nice place, the way *I'd* like it to be, with *my* things. Do you understand? I don't want this – a let out cottage down a lane, with Frank at everybody's beck and call, and not two pennies to rub together."

"Well, there'll be a new house," I said, "Frank has it all set up. James O'Connor is to build a new house on the grants, with big windows and all, and we'll all move in there, and then there will be no call for renting this one, and Frank'll save money in the end."

"Oh there will, will there?" she said.

"I told Frank to make it big, so there'd be room for the whole dang pack of us," I said. "And no stairs, because Mammy can't go up them."

"And what if I *want* stairs?" she said, slowly.

I looked at her. She was terrible selfish. Did she know how terrible selfish she was being?

"If you want stairs, I suppose you'll get them," I said. "Just don't ask Mammy to be going up them, will you?"

"I won't," she said, and she lit herself another cigarette, and took three quick puffs at it. Then she started looking at her nails.

"It's half-past two in the morning!" I said. "Did you ever?"

"See what comes of keeping bad company," she said.

"They'll be back soon," I said.

"I'm sure they will," she said.

"Mike can bed down on the sofa, and I'll take the chair with my bedspread," I said.

"*Mike!*" she said. "He knows what he can go and do."

"Well, he can't go and do it up the lane in the middle of the night, for fear he'd wake Mammy," I said, by-the-way making light of it. I could see she was mad at Mike for getting in trouble with the police, and dragging our name in the mud.

"It would never do to wake *Mammy* up!" said Carmel.

"That's right," I said. She was on edge, I could see that. She'd got up, and she was walking round the room, puffing at the cigarette.

"It would never do to cross *Mammy!*" she said.

I didn't say anything. The late night was fairly loosening Carmel's tongue for her.

"Do you know something?" Carmel said. "Do you know that Teresa one? Do you know she could be married and in Australia these long years? She was asked, but she wouldn't go. And you know why she wouldn't go? You know who wouldn't let her?"

"Mammy?" I said. It was the first time I'd heard tell of anyone asking Teresa that class of a question.

"Right!" said Carmel. "Only Teresa's man, the one that asked her, he had the right idea. He wasn't staying round here, to have his wife at *her* beck and call, up the lane. He had it sized up. 'Come with me to Australia, Teresa,' he said, but would she go? Would she hell!"

"Maybe she didn't like him," I said. I couldn't imagine Teresa getting off with a man at all.

"Didn't she just!" said Carmel. "Oh, she liked him all right."

"Then she should have married him," I said.

"There's one up there who doesn't want *anybody* married," said Carmel. "Anybody at all. Frank or Rose or Teresa or your Mike, even if anyone would have them – she doesn't want them married, because if they're married it's not 'our ones', is it? It's strangers getting in. She wants 'our ones' and 'our place' all dancing round herself till she steps off into the next world."

"You shouldn't talk like that," I said. "You were made welcome."

"*Welcome!*" said Carmel.

"Yes."

"She wouldn't let me in the house till Frank stood up to her," said Carmel. "He told her right to her face, and that put paid to her game."

I didn't say anything. Maybe Mammy was right about Carmel, and her lies. Twisting everything round so it sounded right. It wasn't like that at all. It was Carmel got her hooks in Frank, and he wouldn't pay heed when he was warned what she'd turn out to be.

There was the sound of a car in the lane, and it pulled into the yard.

"Put out that cigarette before Frank sees it," I told Carmel, but she didn't do it. I knew Frank would be mad if he caught her, but there is no telling some people.

The car door slammed, and a moment or two later Frank came into the house.

"Where's Mike?" I said.

"I left him down there," Frank said. "Sleeping it off."

"And the other fella?" Carmel said.

"Begley?" said Frank. "He'll live."

"What Begley is that?" I said, quickly, for I'd got the message all right. Mike must have laid into Rose's man, for doing that to her.

"Begley the scrap-man," Frank said. "You'll know all about him soon enough." He went off to the bedroom.

"There you are now," Carmel said, getting up to follow him.

I wanted to know, instead of just working things out by myself, so I plunged straight in.

"Carmel," I said. "Is Begley ... I mean, is Begley the scrap-man the one that did *that* to Rose?"

Carmel stopped, like she was hit with a stone.

"The baby, I mean," I said. "The baby Rose is having. Is Begley the father?"

"Yes," said Carmel, without moving.

"Begley is the daddy?" I said again.

"*Yes,*" Carmel said, and then she bit her lip, in an embarrassed way. "But he ... he isn't *your* daddy, pet."

"What?" I said. "*My* daddy? How could he be?"

"Oh Jesus! Me and my big mouth," Carmel said, and she turned round and bolted into the bedroom, slamming the door behind her.

I stood there, gaping after her.

Frank came out, and he came over to me, and put his arm round me.

"She didn't mean it, Kathleen," he said. "She didn't mean any harm. It just slipped out of her."

"I don't understand," I said, but a part of me did. I could feel tears brimming up in me.

Frank gave me a big hug.

"You're not to think too badly of Rose," he said. "She was only a wee girl like yourself when it happened."

"I don't understand," I repeated.

"*Frank!*" Carmel called from the bedroom. "Frank, come in here."

He went like a dog with its tail between its legs.

I just sat there, tugging at my bedspread.

Frank came out again.

"Carmel says we'll talk about it in the morning," he said, avoiding my eye. "Carmel says the whole thing is between you and Rose, and it should have been Rose who told you. Carmel says she's awful sorry, and she didn't mean any harm."

"Och aye," I said. "Carmel says."

"Rose'll talk to you in the morning," Frank said.

He went to hug me again, but I moved off him.

I didn't want hugging or anything.

98

I just wanted to be by my own self, until I could understand.

"You let a stranger tell me!" I said. "Could somebody not have told me before? Does everyone know except me?"

"*Kathleen*," he said, awkwardly. The big idiot, could he not say it straight out, and make things easier for me?

"Mammy is not my mammy at all?" I said. "You're telling me that? Mammy is not my mammy, and Rose is?"

"That's it," he said.

"Who is my daddy, then?" I said.

"You'll need to talk to Rose about that," he said. "It had better come from Rose."

"You never told me," I said. "*None* of you ever told me!"

He stood there looking at me, like he didn't know what to say next.

"Kathleen," he said. "Kathleen!"

"Just leave well alone!" I said, and I ran down the hall to the bathroom, and got in there, and got the door banged and locked behind me.

I didn't want anybody with me.

I sat and I sat in there, and I could hear them at it in the living-room, but I didn't go out. There was a knock on the door, and Carmel started on about me not staying there all night.

"Just leave me be," I told her.

Frank came and rattled the handle and spoke my name, and then he said would I not come out,

99

and then I said I wouldn't, and then they went off and had another slanging match.

"We're off to bed, Kathleen," Carmel called through the door.

"Aye," I said.

"Will you not come out to the sofa?"

"No," I said.

There was a pause.

"You'd not do anything silly?"

"No."

She went away.

I didn't come out for ages, until I was sure the coast was clear. Then I huddled down under my rainbow bedspread on Carmel's posh sofa like somebody's wee baby, in its cot.

CHAPTER ELEVEN

I was up early in the morning, because I couldn't face Carmel or Frank.

I got dressed, and went up to our house, and then I got the photographs down off the shelf.

Me, being christened. I looked at the photograph a long time. Mammy was holding me in the photograph, and Rose had her hand out, adjusting the wrap. Teresa was standing back, with a face on her.

Mammy and Rose.

Mammy was an old woman in the photograph. Fifteen years ago. And Daddy wasn't there, because Daddy was dead then, and even before he was dead he wasn't at home for nearly a year.

I looked at Daddy's photograph, and his short dark hair. Dark, like all the family – and me thinking my fair hair was just a throwback!

Daddy wasn't Daddy, and Mammy wasn't Mammy. Rose was my mammy. Our Rose.

I wanted to go upstairs to her, but I didn't. Instead, I went out to the barn, and up to my own place, to pretend I was a mouse again.

I half scared the life out of an old hen!

The swans were on the lake.

They have a nest in the reeds, the swans, and they were out with a trail of wee ones behind them. The mammy and the daddy and the wee ones.

The heat of the hay came up into me. In the first of the day the sun comes in the barn, it is later on that it is a shady place.

Rose was my mammy.

How could I go all these years and not know it? How could they not tell me? I suppose it's one of those things people don't say. But *somebody* should have. *Rose* should have. She'd know I'd find out – maybe she was going to tell me and then just couldn't do it. That would be like Rose. Maybe she hoped Mammy would do it, or Teresa, but it was down to her, really. Her personal private business, nobody else's. You couldn't expect the others to do it for her. I wasn't crying about that. I don't know what I was crying about, but I had a cry anyway.

You can't go on crying. I got out of the barn, sliding down the bales, and I went across the yard and down the low field towards the lake.

The swans looked at me, but they didn't come near.

I went to Daddy's rock.

One time, when Teresa was small, she went in a

bog hole. Mammy says that Daddy was in the field, and he saw her, and he was over the ground like an Olympic sprinter. He got her out, or she would have been down in the churchyard, with our Bernie.

When I was a wee girl, I used to make-believe talk to Bernie before Rose came up to bed at night.

Bernadette Fay.

She was my *auntie*. She wasn't my sister at all.

I lay down in the grass, and I thought about her.

If she could come back, and walk down the lake by me, what would she think of me, and all our ones?

Would she be ashamed of me, and what I was – what I *knew* I was, now?

I knew what she'd think.

She'd be like Mike and me and Rose, fit for a laugh, even when there was blue murder going on. Just like me and Rose in the lane, with no jobs and no money and the house knocked down, laughing our heads off.

You have to see things are funny. You'd never get through life at all if you couldn't see the funny side.

The new baby would be my sister, when it was born. Or brother – but somehow I was sure it was a sister. And I'd help Rose with it, the way I helped Carmel with Imelda. Only it would be different. Everything was going to be different. How could it not all be different?

"Kathleen?" Ann said.

She'd walked up on me, without my knowing. She must have seen me out of O'Connor's big window, looking out on the lake.

"Hi," I said.

She sat down beside me.

"Anything wrong?" she said.

"Yes," I said.

"What?" she said.

"You know our Rose is having a baby?" I said.

"Yes," she said.

"You know Rose is my mammy too?" I said, not looking at her.

"Yes," she said.

"Well, that's what is wrong," I said.

Ann didn't say anything.

"I suppose everybody round here knows?" I said. "About me, and Rose being my mammy, I mean?"

"I suppose they do," said Ann, unhappily.

"The Kiltarragh bike," I said. "That's what they call her, isn't it?"

"That's a horrible name," Ann said.

"Why did she do it, Ann?" I said. "Why did she go round … you know…"

"Doing what comes naturally!" said Ann, trying to make a laugh of it, but catching on halfway that it was no joke.

"It's *awful*," I said.

"No, it's not," Ann said. "If I lived here I – well, there's not much else to do, is there?"

I gave her a look.

"I thought you knew," Ann said, hopelessly.

"Auntie Mary said you *must* know, by now."

"I'm a right fool," I said.

"It's not so bad," Ann said.

"It's not you it's happening to," I said.

She shrugged. "There's not much you can do about it, is there? It isn't *happening,* anyway. It all happened a long time ago."

"I can do something," I said. "I can get away from here."

"But you don't really want to," Ann said. "You know you don't. I've tried to talk you into it before now."

"Before was different," I said. "I couldn't stay on here with everybody knowing."

"Everybody has always known," she said. "Well, almost everybody."

That only made it worse.

"I'm going back to the house to tell them," I said, standing up.

"Hold on," Ann said. "Hold on a minute."

"What for?"

"You need to think it over."

I shook my head.

"Well, look, do you want me to walk up with you?" she said. "You can't go up there looking like that, with your face all red."

"I can go where I want, with my face any old way!" I told her, and I walked off.

She didn't come after me.

Halfway round by the lake, I got some water and splashed my face, so my eyes wouldn't give me away. I didn't want to please them by letting them see I'd been crying.

I went on up the field, and clambered up on to the wall, where I had a look back to see if Ann was watching me. If she'd run back to have a gossip with her auntie about the fool I was, then so much the worse for her.

Ann was still sitting on the rock. She gave me a wave.

I let on I didn't see her.

Somebody rapped on the window at me.

It was Mammy.

I went in to her.

She'd be wanting her leg done, first thing, as usual.

"Child dear," she said. "What's got into you? Your nose is blue!"

"It's cool out there," I said.

She gave me a mug of tea, and I sat there drinking it, wondering where had my big scene gone. Coming up the field I'd had it all worked out, but now…

Frank came into the kitchen, and caught sight of me.

"There you are!" he said.

"Here I am," I said, looking him straight in the eye, and challenging him to say something.

"You're all right?" he said.

"I'm all right," I said.

"Why wouldn't she be?" said Mammy, sharply.

I knew why he was worried. He was afraid I'd

let on to Mammy that it was Carmel who let the cat out of the bag about Rose and me.

"Mike's not back?" Frank said.

"What's wrong with Mike?" said Mammy, rising to the bait.

And Frank told her.

I slipped out of the room.

Cheated of my big scene!

Rose and Teresa were out the back, seeing to the pigs.

I thought for a minute I would go to Rose, and say what Carmel said, and then I didn't know how to say it, and I slipped off back to the barn, and my own hidey-hole, where nobody could get at me.

Frank could tell them, in his own time.

CHAPTER TWELVE

Mike came back, rattling into the yard in Frank's old car.

He didn't see me in my hidey-hole.

His suit was all crumpled, and he looked a mess. He is a mess, anyway. I'd been thinking about him, and wondering if he'd take me with him, back to London, but deep down I knew I wouldn't go.

He'd got away from Kiltarragh all right, but he'd never left. Kiltarragh was always there, somewhere he could run back to when he was on his uppers, with a box of sticky sweets for the child, and a Spanish lace shawl for Mammy. Not that it was Spanish lace anyway, for Teresa had spotted the label, and showed me. The shawl was made in Hong Kong. Our big city man was a fake!

Frank was waiting for him, at the door.

"You're back," Frank said.

"I am," said Mike, rubbing his hands. "I am, and I've done what needed doing."

"You're in fine song this morning," said Frank. "You weren't so great last night."

"I was man enough for Begley," said Mike.

"You have no sense!" said Frank, sounding wild.

"If Begley messes around with my sister, he has it coming to him," said Mike.

Mammy had to take Mike's part, as usual. She'd come out of the door, and now she flared up for the prodigal son.

"If there was one here man enough to do it, it would have been done long since," she said. "It took our Mike here to do it,"

"Begley's a randy git," said Mike. "Messing in the back seat of his car with my sister."

"It takes two to tango," said Frank.

I'd slipped down to the door of the barn, where I could get a better look.

Mammy spotted me. She has eyes in the back of her head where I'm concerned.

"*You!*" she said. "Out of it."

I headed for the wall.

"Right out and away from it!" said Mammy. "No hanging around."

I hopped over the wall.

Frank and Mike were yelling at each other, but I couldn't make out what they were saying, and what I could make out I wouldn't repeat.

Then I heard Rose.

She was shouting too, and then she let a squeal out of her, as if she'd been hit.

I put my head up over the wall.

Rose was up against the window, holding her face, and Mike was after her – or he would have been if Frank hadn't grabbed him.

"I'll hang for you, Mike!" Frank said, and the next minute he had Mike against the house wall, banging his head.

Mammy grabbed hold of Frank.

"Leave go of me till I finish this London cowboy off!" Frank shouted, but she wouldn't. She yanked Frank off, though he was twice the size of her.

"Bastard!" Mike said. His mouth was bleeding so Frank must have hit him. There was blood down his shirt.

He staggered to his feet, looking as if he was going to murder Frank.

Mammy got in between them again, and started giving off at Frank.

They were in the middle of it when Begley's car came up the lane. I knew it must be Begley's, because it was the Renault that had been here before, and there was a man in it with a big bruise on his lip.

Mike had got him, all right!

The car pulled up in front of the house, and Begley got out.

It was the first time I'd had a good look at him, and he wasn't much.

He was like a boiled spud. A round man, in a grey suit, with his shirt apart where the trousers met the buttons, so that you could see his blue vest.

He was no oil painting, and the swelling round his mouth didn't help.

"I'm here for Rose," he announced, getting out of the car.

Where was Rose? I didn't know, and she wasn't in the yard any more. She must have run off after Mike hit her.

"Rose is going nowhere," Mammy said.

"You're asking for more of the same, Begley," Mike said, his face pale, with blood trickling from his teeth.

Begley stood his ground.

"I want to see my Rose!" he said.

"Get off our land!" Mike roared at him. "You dirty bugger. Get your feet and your car off our land this minute, or I'll have you in the Daisy Hill." From the look of Mike the hospital was where Begley was headed.

"You lay another hand on that man, and you'll have me to answer to," Frank said, rounding on Mike.

I thought Mike was going to hit him.

"I've come to take Rose away with me," Begley said, bravely enough, although he looked frightened out of his fat skin.

"Rose is going nowhere!" Mammy said, for the second time.

"Oh, but Rose *is*," Rose said, coming out of the house. She walked over to Begley's car, and got into the front seat.

"Come on, Sean," she said.

111

"Get outa that car!" Mammy ordered her.

"I'm sorry to be on your wrong side, Mrs Fay," Begley said. "But Rose is coming with me, and that is all there is to it."

"*You*—" Mike roared, but Frank grabbed him, and hauled him back against the wall.

Begley got in the car and started the engine, though it took him two goes. Rose sat there beside him, staring straight in front of her.

"You're no daughter of mine, Rose Fay!" Mammy shouted at her, and she ran over and banged the glass of the car window, but the window didn't break.

Begley started her up, and swung the car into the lane.

"I'll *kill* the git!" Mike shouted, and he struggled clear of Frank, and picked up a stone which he heaved after the car. It blattered down on the rusty blue roof, denting it.

"Mike!" Mammy said. "Mike!"

She'd gone over on the ground when the car took off. Now she was sitting there, all the fight gone out of her.

Mike didn't hear her. He was still roaring and ranting after the car. It was Frank who got her up on her feet and then Teresa came and helped her back into the house.

Frank went over to Mike.

"I don't want you about the place," he said. "You can get your things and clear off."

Mike just stared at him.

112

"Who is saying that?" he said, after a moment.

"I am," said Frank. "And what I say goes."

"We'll see about that," said Mike, and he went into the house.

Frank just stood there. Then he turned round and saw me, before I could duck down behind the wall.

"Kathleen?" he called to me.

I couldn't speak to him.

I just turned and ran, away down the field towards the lake.

Frank didn't come after me.

CHAPTER THIRTEEN

"Kathleen?" Teresa said.

"Hi," I said.

She'd put on her boots to come and get me, across the low field. I don't know how she found me, for I was down in the wet grass hoping no one would see me.

"You can't stay out here for ever, Kathleen," she said.

"Can't I?" I said. "Why not?"

The way I felt I wasn't ever going back to the house. Not after all that carry-on. Not after what they'd done to Rose.

"Sean Begley's not a *bad* man, Kathleen," she said. "He's … he's maybe not all he might be, but there's nobody perfect. Anybody can make a mistake. Sean Begley will look after her. He's not a bad man."

"I don't want it to be like this," I said, with a choky feeling inside me, not wanting to be crying again. What's the use of crying, when the milk is spilt?

"It was Mike mucked things up, Kathleen," she said. "It would have been all right if he hadn't come back from England to knock Sean Begley's head off. Frank had everything arranged with the Begleys."

"*All right!*" I said, wondering if she knew what all right was. It could never be all right, never again.

"Frank will still sort it all out with Begley, Kathleen," Teresa said.

"What about Mammy?" I said.

"Mammy will have to learn to live with it," said Teresa. "Now, come on back to the house. They're all worrying about you."

"No," I said. "Not yet."

"Why not?"

"Just no," I said. I didn't know why not. Kiltarragh is my own place, but I just didn't know whether it was or not any more. I didn't know where I belonged, or who I belonged with.

"You can't stay out here," she said. "I tell you what, we'll go down to Carmel's, will we? Then you can have a cup of tea, and a talk."

I didn't want to go to Carmel's, but I went. Teresa made me. Like Ann said, Teresa really is great nun material. She reminded me of Sister Attracta at school – gentle all the way, but standing no fuss.

I was too tired and upset to argue with her anyroad – and what else could I do, for I had

115

nowhere to go.

Carmel was down there, and Imelda. Teresa and Carmel had a long talk in the kitchen, and then they went back up to the house to speak to Frank, leaving me in the kitchen with the child.

"The two babies together," I told Imelda, and we put on Carmel's TV and watched the cartoons, and *World at One* on the BBC.

Then Teresa came in, with her coat on.

"Where are you heading?" I asked, because I wanted to know what was happening, and nobody was telling me anything – as usual.

"I'm driving Mike down to Dundalk, to the station," she said. "He's off on his travels again, leaving the rest of us to pick up the pieces."

"He's not going for good?" I said, because I didn't want him to be. Mike's not a bad person, even if he does fly off the handle.

"He'll be back, like a bad penny," said Teresa.

She drove off with Mike. He gave me a £5 note through the car window when I went out to God bless him, but he was awkward about it, as if he didn't know what to say to me.

"We'll think about your trip to London, Kathleen," he said. "Maybe another time? I could do with the company."

"Maybe," I said, although I'd already made up my mind about that.

Off they went.

I went back into the house and told Imelda stories, but my heart wasn't in the Starry Nights.

How could it be?

Frank came, when we were in the middle of meeting the Wise Salmon in our lake.

"Rose wants to talk to you," he told me.

"Is she here?" I said, looking for her.

"She's in the town, waiting," Frank said.

"Not at Sean Begley's?"

"Neutral ground, eh?" Frank said. "She just wants a word. But listen, Kathleen. You're not to be too hard on her."

"Why would I be?" I said.

He didn't answer that one.

He just said: "She loves you, Kathleen, you know that. You're her wee girl, and she loves you more than any living thing."

CHAPTER FOURTEEN

It wasn't Frank who took me to meet Rose, it was Carmel. Frank had to stay, for the cow was calving. That's what he said, anyway.

I didn't care. After the first upset, and the tears, something had gone cold inside me. I was hurt enough.

Carmel had some of Rose's things in the back for her, and the arrangement was that we'd meet at Mooney's Hotel, in the Main Street.

It's just a bar, really, not a proper hotel.

Begley's blue Renault was parked by the pumps outside when we got there, and Rose and Begley were in the lounge bar, round the side from the hall.

Begley got up when I came in.

"This is Kathleen, Sean," Rose said. "And my sister-in-law, Carmel."

"Can I get anybody a drink?" Begley said, when he had shaken our hands. He had big strong hands, for a small man.

"No, indeed," said Carmel, quickly. "I'll need to be getting back. Perhaps you could help me move Rose's things from the car, Mr Begley?"

I looked at Carmel. She wasn't going to leave me, was she?

"Sean," Begley said. "You can call me Sean, daughter, now we're all going to be in the family."

"Daughter" is just a way of talking round here, but she could have been his daughter. He was old enough – far too old for Rose, even if he was her last chance saloon.

They went away to Carmel's car.

"How is Mammy?" Rose asked, sitting there on the bar seat, twiddling her lemonade shandy.

"I didn't see her," I said. "I wanted away from everybody for a bit, until I could work things out."

"I'm … I'm sorry, Kathleen," she said.

"*You* should have told me," I said.

"That's easy said!" she said.

I shouldn't have gone at her like that. She was all in pieces anyway.

"I'm sorry too," I said, but still I couldn't keep the edge of bitterness out of my voice. Everybody knew, everybody in the place knew what I was, and they'd all been talking about me and thinking that about me all those years, and never a word had anybody said to *me*, the one it mattered most to.

"It's going to be better from now on, Kathleen," Rose said. "Sean is a decent man, and he has a place we can go to, just the three of us."

"You, and Sean, and the baby," I said.

There was a long silence. She put down her glass.

"I wasn't thinking about the baby," she said.

I bit back what I might have said – *having* babies was her strong suit.

"You'll like it, Kathleen," she said. "Honest you will. Sean has a new bungalow—"

"The one with the rusty cars round it, on the Scarratstown Road," I said. I'd look a fine princess picking my way through scrap iron and old tyres to the front door of my palace!

"It's not the best, maybe," Rose admitted. "But Sean has plans. And we can make it good. We'll make a home of it, for all of us. And that means you as well, Kathleen."

"Starry Nights!" I said. Did she not know how I was inside? It was no time for dream stories. Her hunky prince was an old man with a beer paunch and her palace was a breeze-block shack at the side of a scrapyard, could she not see that?

"We *can* make it good," she said, understanding what I meant well enough, but afraid to face up to it. Maybe she wasn't afraid. Maybe having a Starry Night story about it was the only way she could face it.

"You're my daughter, Kathleen," she said.

"Begley isn't my father!" I snapped back. Then I had a bad thought. Maybe he *was*. He couldn't be, could he? "He isn't, is he?" I said, anxiously, and she must have known from the way I said it what I thought about him.

"No," she said.

There was a long silence.

"Well?" I said.

It was time I knew. Long gone time. I couldn't walk around the countryside looking at all the men with mousy hair, wondering which one was my father, could I?

Then I said a thing I shouldn't have.

"I suppose you do *know*?"

She gave me a look like the cow gave Imelda, and the colour went out of her cheeks. I thought she was going to start crying on me, but she didn't. Why shouldn't she cry? I'd done enough crying already for the two of us, up in my hidey-hole and out in the field.

"I was only a wee girl like you, Kathleen," she said.

Oh no, I thought. *Not like me*. There was no way I'd end up in that boat, with no oarsman.

"All I want to know is who he is," I said.

"He was a fine fella," she said.

"He wasn't that fine, or he would have married you," I said.

Why was I hurting her? She had it all to answer for, that's why. I could hear myself doing it, but I couldn't help it. The words kept coming out of me.

"He went away, your daddy did," she said.

"Was he married already?" I said, straight out.

"I suppose he was," she said.

"Don't you know?"

"He told me he was," she said. "He wrote and told me, after he was away. It was a lovely letter, Kathleen. A lovely letter. How he'd keep in touch and everything."

"And did he?" I said.

"I expect he got in some old bother," she said. "He would have if he could. I know he would have."

"Did you not write to him?" I said, impatient with her. "Did you not tell him about me, and everything?"

"How could I?" she said.

"Easily," I said.

"Where would I write to?" she said.

"I don't get you," I said.

"How would I know where he'd be?"

"You'd write to the address on his letter," I said.

"There was no address on his letter."

"But..."

"I only knew him a wee while, Kathleen," she said.

"Long enough!" I said.

"He was passing through," she said. "Just passing through in his van."

"A bagman!" I said, bitterly. My daddy was a bagman, passing through.

"It was an awful nice letter, Kathleen," she said, hopelessly.

I sat there, not saying anything. My daddy, the fine man, was just another Starry Night she'd made for herself, out of somebody who'd taken her out up some laneway in his van, and left her in the lurch.

Well, at least now I knew.

"At least you know his name?" I said.

"Donal," she said.

"Donal who?" I said.

"Donal somebody-or-other," she said. "I couldn't read his writing."

I let that one sink in.

"After he was gone, you came along," she said. That seemed to me to be kind of *obvious*. "And Mammy and Teresa and Frank and Mike and me all loved you, and we brought you up in the house, like the rest of us, because that is what you are, Kathleen, whatever other people round here may call you."

We stopped talking.

There was a fish tank behind the bar, with a green fish and a blue fish in it, and a plastic diver in a diver's suit, helmet and all. Above it there was the Starry Plough, that Mike told me was our *real* flag, the flag of Ireland, Protestant and Catholic together.

"You're making it hard for me, Kathleen," Rose said.

"I'm sorry," I said.

"If you'd just come out and see the house…" she began.

"I don't know what I'm going to do," I said. "I need to think about it."

She gave me a hug.

"I want to go back home now," I said, standing up. "Back to Kiltarragh."

Why did I want to hurt her? She only loved me. Hadn't she done all she could for me, since I was a wee child, like Imelda? She should have told me though – some of them could have told me, so that I'd know.

I drove back in the car with Carmel, thinking about it.

The army stopped us, just before the Cross. They had Carmel and me out on the roadside, and they searched the boot, and then they let us go. One of them tried to joke us, but we never said a word to please them.

"That makes me mad," I said, when we were going again. I wanted to talk about something – *anything* – that wasn't about me. I couldn't talk to Carmel about me. She was just a stranger. I couldn't talk about *me,* and I couldn't stand the silence in the car, and her prune face.

"It is the way things are," Carmel said. I think she was relieved to be talking too.

"So long as the Brits are here," I said.

"They're only poor fellas off the streets of Liverpool," Carmel said. "It isn't their problem."

"So long as they are here, it is," I said. "They should get out of our country."

"Here we go again," she said.

"Well, that's it," I said. "That's what the boys

are fighting for."

"What for?"

"For Ireland!" I said.

"Then God save Ireland from them!" Carmel said, snappily enough. "Songs in pubs, and soldiers in the hedge, and every man a hero."

"Don't let Frank hear you say that," I said.

"Frank's a farmer, Kathleen," she said. "He minds his business. One day, if this goes on, he'll likely get shot by one side or the other. It is time you knocked all that nonsense out of your head, before somebody gets hurt by it."

I shut up, because I wasn't going to talk to her about it.

"People have to get by, day to day, Kathleen," she said. "All the other stuff is just dreams."

"Ideals," I said. "There's people round here have died for their ideals."

"They'd be better off working for them," she said. "Dying is easy. You don't have to think much about it. You just plant a bomb and get yourself shot, and the next thing you are a holy martyr for Ireland."

"Not everybody's clever," I said. "Somebody's got to do the fighting, or the Brits will never go."

"Who'll you fight, *then*?" she said.

"When?"

"When the Brits go," she said. "*If* the Brits go. Will you fight the Protestants?"

"If we have to," I said.

"And when you've finished that?" she said.

"Who'll you fight then? Somebody else that doesn't happen to agree with you?"

"There won't be anybody else," I said.

"Oh yes, there will," Carmel said. "There's always somebody else, Kathleen. Somebody else with different dreams that they call ideals, for if there wasn't, you'd have nothing to fight about, would you? And nobody to kill."

I was dang glad to get out of the car, I can tell you. I think Carmel was too.

We went into Carmel's house, and Carmel went to see to Imelda. Frank was there, and we had a long talk on the sofa about Rose.

"Maybe Sean Begley and Rose could come and live with us in the new house, when you have it built?" I said.

"Maybe," he said, but I knew he didn't mean it.

CHAPTER FIFTEEN

The next morning I went up to our house and did Mammy's leg, and then I went off across the fields to O'Connor's, to say goodbye to Ann. She was going back to Belfast.

"Well?" she said.

"Rose wants me to go and live with her, in Sean Begley's bungalow at the scrapyard," I said. "Me, on the scrap-heap!"

"What are you going to do?" Ann asked.

"I don't know," I said, looking out of the big picture window at the lake. There was a cold wind blowing, and a grey sky. The lake was dark.

"I know what I would do," she said. "If you stay at Kiltarragh, you'll get like them, Teresa and Frank, tied to the old woman's apron strings."

"Frank has Carmel," I said. I didn't like to hear Ann or anyone else talking about Mammy like that.

"Frank has no life of his own," Ann said.

"I don't know Sean Begley or his ones," I said.

"I don't know how I'd manage living in his place when I don't know him and I don't know it, and I wouldn't know who I was."

"You're *you*," she said. "The place you're in needn't make you, unless you let it."

"Come again?" I said, not quite sure what she meant. Anyway, I didn't feel strong. I was just a pass-the-parcel for everybody to play with.

"Never mind, Kathleen," she said. "Look, it is only down the road you're going to. You're not talking about New York. You can come back to Kiltarragh and see them all if you want to."

"It wouldn't be the same," I said.

"*You* wouldn't be the same," she said. "Either you get out from under and make a life for yourself – here or somewhere else – or you sit still, and let other people make you into what they want you to be."

That was what she meant about Teresa and Frank.

"Up at Kiltarragh, old Mrs Fay rules the roost," Ann said. "I couldn't put up with it."

I felt like telling her it *was* Mammy's roost. Her house, and her land, and the life she brought us all into. Well, not me, but she was Rose's mammy, and I'm the granddaughter, so I was part and parcel of it.

"You can let Kiltarragh swallow you up, if you want to," Ann said. "Or you can begin to think for yourself. It doesn't matter where you live, Kathleen, or who you're with. The problem is the same. You can make your own life, or you can go around in a life someone has made up for you, off the peg. And if it doesn't fit you – well, you'll have to put up with it."

Ann had to go.

She went off up North, in James O'Connor's big car.

I waved at her until she was gone, and then I walked back by the lake, and sat down on Daddy's rock, looking up at our house, with the black plastic window like a patch on its eye.

Two grey wagons buzzed down the Scarrat-stown Road, with their soldiers in them, regimental flags flying, guns peeping out the back. They'd be there for ever, just like me, doing what they were told to do.

The wagons turned left at Cone Cross, past the bomb crater, and on to town, where there would be no welcome for them, just the fish trapped in their tank, and the Starry Plough flag in Mooney's bar.

For the first time in my life I found myself wondering what it would be like to be one of *them* – a Brit, or a Protestant like the ones Ann met in Belfast. They'd have their own ideas, the Brits and the Protestants, and their own dreams. They'd be different dreams from ours – from mine – but where had I got my dreams from? Maybe the dreams were getting in my way, making me be somebody I wasn't. Maybe the dreams were just a trap.

Maybe they were, but life would be awful difficult

without them.

Without them, I'd have to start at the beginning, with every dang thing, and work out what really mattered. Then I wouldn't be Rose's baby, or Mammy's granddaughter, or Kiltarragh's child. I'd just be me.

I looked up at the house again.

Teresa was out in the yard, in her apron. She must have seen me. She gave me a wave.

Were they afraid I was so upset that I'd throw myself in the old, cold lake? If that was it, Kiltarragh didn't know its own daughter.

Turn around a time, and Mammy would be dead.

Turn around another, and Teresa would be like her.

And me?

What would I be?

The swans went by on the lake, two big ones and a clatter of little ones.

I went off back to the house thinking that from that day on I'd be myself, if I was strong enough to be it.

I went back to Kiltarragh, because it seemed as good a place as any to begin, and if I couldn't manage it there, then I'd try somewhere else.

NOTES FOR *STARRY NIGHT,*
FRANKIE'S STORY AND *THE BEAT OF THE DRUM*

I have been asked to explain some of the terms used in these books to help readers who are not familiar with the Northern Ireland situation. These notes are not intended to be comprehensive, nor can they possibly deal with the finer points of Irish history or politics. People, events and organizations who don't appear in the books don't make it into the notes either. The intent is simply to make the problems faced by Kathleen, Frankie and Brian easier to understand.

HISTORY AND GEOGRAPHY

Ireland – The island of Ireland is made up of thirty-two counties. Historically the country, which was ruled by the British for many centuries, was divided into four provinces, one of which is Ulster.

Ulster – The province of Ulster consists of nine counties. When partition of Ireland was imposed by the British in 1921 after the War of Independence, three of the nine Ulster counties were part of the newly created Irish Free State which later became the Republic of Ireland.

The *Republic of Ireland* is an independent country with a large Catholic majority.

Northern Ireland consists of the remaining six counties of the province of Ulster. It has a Protestant majority. At present it remains part of the *United Kingdom of Great Britain and Northern Ireland*.

GLOSSARY

Terms used when speaking of both sides:

Paramilitary – In present-day Northern Ireland this term is used to describe terrorist organizations, either Protestant or Catholic, who are prepared to kill to further their own political ends.

Terms used when speaking of the Irish side:

Catholic – The religion of the vast majority of the population of Ireland as a whole, and of a substantial minority of the population of Northern Ireland.

Nationalist – Those who desire a thirty-two-county united Ireland. Many, but by no means all, Catholics in Northern Ireland are Nationalists.

SDLP – The Social Democrat and Labour Party. The main Nationalist Party in Northern Ireland. The SDLP supports the unification of Ireland by democratic means, but is totally opposed to the use of force to achieve this end.

Republican Movement – The minority within the Nationalist community in Northern Ireland who very largely support the use of armed force to achieve a united Ireland.

Republican Areas – Areas regarded by Protestants as strongholds of Catholics who support the Republican Movement.

Fenian – Historically an Irish warrior. An abusive term when used by Protestants, meaning Catholic and implying rebel.

IRA – Historically the paramilitary wing of the Republican Movement.

The Provisional IRA/Provos/ Provies – The main paramilitary wing of present-day Republicanism, which was initially a splinter group of the IRA, but has now virtually superseded that organization. The term IRA is often used to describe the Provisional IRA.

Sinn Fein – A political party which supports the aims and ideals of the Provisional IRA. Believed by many Unionists to be one and the same with that organization.

Gerry Adams – President of Sinn Fein.

Terms used when speaking of the British side:

Protestant – The religion of the majority of the population of Northern Ireland, many of whom are of Scots and English descent.

Unionists – Those who support the union of Great Britain with Northern Ireland. Many, but by no means all, Protestants in Northern Ireland are Unionists.

RUC – The Royal Ulster Constabulary. The police force in Northern Ireland is largely Protestant. Attempts are being made, not very successfully, to redress this imbalance. Catholics who join the RUC are very vulnerable to Republican attack. Protestant paramilitaries who oppose government policy regard the RUC as traitors to their cause.

UDR – The Ulster Defence Regiment was a locally recruited and mainly Protestant unit of the British Army. Now replaced by the Royal Irish Regiment.

Loyalists – The hard edge of Protestant Unionism. Many, but by no means all, Loyalists are prepared to use force to maintain the union with Great Britain, and some are willing to fight the British to prove it.

UDA – The Ulster Defence Association. A Protestant organization with some political and some paramilitary overtones.

UFF – Ulster Freedom Fighters. A Protestant paramilitary organization, believed by many to be part of the UDA.

UVF – Ulster Volunteer Force. A Protestant paramilitary organization.

The Orange Order –
A Protestant religious
organization with political and
charitable overtones. It has
considerable influence within
Unionist politics.

The Twelfth – 12 July.
The Orange Order's annual
celebration of the victory of the
Protestant King William of
Orange (King Billy) over the
Catholic King James II at the
Battle of the Boyne in 1690.
Orange Order Marches take
place all over Northern Ireland
and many fiery speeches are
made.

"The Sash" – "The Sash my
Father Wore" is an Orange
Order marching song. The sash
referred to in the song is a
form of collarette worn by
Orangemen on parade.

The Ulster Red Hand flag –
The Red Hand is the traditional
symbol of Ulster.

THE BEAT OF THE DRUM
Martin Waddell

Brian Hanna doesn't hate the Catholics.

Even though, in the eyes of the Loyalists, he's got good reason – having been left disabled since infancy by the IRA bomb that killed his parents. What he does hate is the mindless bigotry that justifies the bloodshed on both sides, and the way that men of violence manipulate people to further their cause. But can Brian break free from the beat of the drums?

The Beat of the Drum is one of a trilogy of powerful and moving stories set in eighties Northern Ireland.

"Deals passionately and poignantly with the contemporary Ulster 'troubles'." *The Irish Times*

FRANKIE'S STORY
Martin Waddell

The writing is on the wall in Unity Park estate.

And it warns that enemies of the Republican cause will not be tolerated. Frankie has lived on the estate her whole life, but now her Protestant boyfriend and her loud opinions on sectarian violence have started to get her a reputation. Shunned by her own community and facing a hate campaign that's getting dangerously out of control, it looks like the writing is on the wall for Frankie.

Frankie's Story is one of a trilogy of powerful and moving stories set in eighties Northern Ireland.

TANGO'S BABY
Martin Waddell

Tango is not one of life's romantic heroes.

Even his friends are amazed to learn of his love affair with young Crystal O'Leary, the girl he fancies and who seemed to have no interest in him. Next thing they know, she's pregnant – and that's when the real story of Tango's baby begins. By turns tragic and farcical, it's a story in which many claim a part, but few are able to help Tango as he strives desperately to keep his new family together.

"Waddell is as ever an excellent storyteller."
The Independent

"Brilliantly written." *The Sunday Telegraph*

THE KIDNAPPING OF SUZIE Q
Martin Waddell

At 4.35 Suzie Quinn is a shopper in her local supermarket. At 4.43 she's a kidnap victim.

One afternoon Suzie Quinn and her mum dash into their local supermarket, planning to be in and out as quickly as possible. Minutes later, while Suzie waits at the checkout, two robbers hold up the store. They too have planned a speedy getaway. But no one has planned for what happens next: after a brief struggle, Suzie finds herself taken hostage by the desperate gang. Now she is Suzie Q, headline kidnap victim, and must summon every ounce of courage and cunning to survive.

This is a dramatic and nail-biting thriller by double Smarties Book Prize Winner, Martin Waddell.

SECOND STAR TO THE RIGHT
Deborah Hautzig

I wouldn't be half bad-looking if I were thin. 5'5½", blue eyes, long light brown hair, small hips – and 125 pounds. If I were thin, my life would be perfect.

On the face of it, Leslie is a normal, healthy, well-adjusted fourteen-year-old girl. She goes to a good school, has a great friend in Cavett, and a mother who loves her to the moon and back. She should be happy, yet she's not. She would be, if only she were thinner. But how thin do you have to be to find happiness?

This is a haunting, honest, utterly compelling account of a girl in the grip of anorexia nervosa.

AND BABY MAKES TWO
Dyan Sheldon

"Happiness was mine. This was what I'd always wanted. Plus, having a baby beat taking my GCSEs."

Lana Spiggs is fed up with everyone telling her what to do – her mother, her teachers... What Lana wants is to be grown up, with her own flat, her own husband and her own children – and no one will be able to boss her around any more.

Then on her fifteenth birthday, Lana meets Les. She knows he's the one and when she gets pregnant, it seems that her wishes are about to come true at last. But can Lana's dream of Happy Families stand up to reality?

By turns funny and hard-hitting, this tale of a teenage mother is a compelling read.

TRIP OF A LIFETIME
Eric Johns

"All this happened to me last summer. I really lost it. It was like I'd blown every circuit in my head."

Mike can't stop thinking about sex. With a mother who gets through men like a monkey polishes off bananas and a dad whose new wife is a nymphomaniac, is it any wonder? Mike's whole life is an emotional seesaw. And then he meets a student nurse who doles out pills like there's no tomorrow... Before he knows it, he's stolen wads of money and is riding happily through the countryside in a horse-drawn caravan.

But is this really the trip of a lifetime or a journey to Hell?